Joyce Kostakis

THE NURSE

Copyright 2024 by Interacting Worlds Press/First Edition
Published: November 21, 2024
ISBN: (paperback) 978-1-7346673-5-6
ISBN: (eBook) 978-1-7346673-6-3
Library of Congress Control Number: 2024919113
COVER: SelfPubBookCovers.com/ andrewgraphics
Edition Date: 12/01/24

Dedication

To my husband Michael. His unwavering encouragement and steadfast support have been the foundation of my journey. He is my compass.

To my favorite sister, Evelyn. She's my only sister, but she knows that if we had another sister, she would still be my favorite. She has perfected the art of sisterhood—the way she listens, laughs and supports me. Through every plot twist, every character arc, she stood by my side, and for that, I am eternally grateful.

To Kathy A. Bates, Ed and Cathy Houston, who brought the short film "The Nurse" to life with their amazing acting skills. Seeing the short film on the big screen inspired me to expand the story into a novel and full feature script. Thank you for all of your encouragement, support, and friendship.

To Nora Carmona, a beacon of guidance and support in my journey. Her belief in me has carried me through every challenge and milestone. I am grateful to have her as a treasured friend in my life.

I didn't write this book alone. To my writers' group that helped me polish the chapters, Cyndi, Ginny, Katelyn, Jacklyn, and Susan, I can't thank you enough for your willingness to read and re-read as I revised the chapters based on your invaluable feedback. It's because of you that this book made it in its final form.

To my editor Nancy and all of my beta readers, I can't thank you enough for your feedback, support, and keen eye when reviewing the chapters. This novel is a tribute to your unwavering support. Your encouragement has been the ink that fills these pages.

Chapter 1 Jill

My watch read ten after five. I took a deep breath, praying my nervousness would leave on the exhale. Running late to our dance lessons for seniors wasn't part of the plan. Jim took longer to get ready these days, and I should have gotten us started earlier. I was still learning how to navigate the impact his diagnosis had on our lives. Today, it was clear I couldn't rush him or get flustered. Both would only slow him down even more.

My hand paused on the recreation room door. I'd have been lying if I said I wasn't worried about the reaction our tardiness would receive. Betty, our instructor, wouldn't start until all the couples had arrived. Our being late stole ten minutes from the hour lesson for the entire group. I figured I might get a few stink eyes but didn't cancel. Dancing was the only thing that made us forget Jim's diagnosis. These precious sixty minutes once a week helped us push back the thoughts of the fog spreading through the crevices of his brain much sooner than either of us expected.

Jim, sensing my hesitation, grabbed my hand and nudged me with his shoulder. We exchanged a smile, then I swung the door open. Our neighborhood recreation room pulsated to the rhythm of Glenn Miller's "In the Mood." The tension I'd been holding drained from my shoulders as the vibration of the music moved through me. Folding chairs lined the sage-green walls. The center of the room, now our makeshift dance hall, would have been empty if not for the six or so other couples practicing their steps. Betty, with her graying red curls pulled up, tapped her foot to the beat.

I waved to everyone with an apologetic smile. No one seemed mad. Eric, a neighbor several streets over, was the only one who didn't smile back. He pretended to brush invisible crumbs from his shirt. His wife, Jess, smiled at us, then returned her attention to Betty.

Betty nodded at our arrival and clapped. "Welcome Jill and Jim. We're all here now. Let's get started. As you all know, I usually make anyone late for class do the recap from the week prior. But…" Her smile widened and with a wink to Jess, she added, "Eric, would you be willing to re-cap last week's lessons with me?"

Jim leaned in and whispered, "Phew, dodged that bullet."

"Yeah, we did."

Betty was being kind by not picking us. I'd warned her Jim may have struggles moving as he declined.

"Do I have to?" Eric whined.

Jess elbowed him.

Eric rolled his eyes and made his way to the center of the room. "Of course, Betty, I'd love to."

Everyone laughed at Eric's reaction. Like many of the husbands, it was clear his wife brought him kicking and screaming.

Betty held her hands in a ready to dance position. "Ex-cellent."

He met her hand with his. "Let's boogie."

Betty threw her head back and laughed. "I think you mean, let's fox-trot. Ready?"

Eric nodded, cheeks reddening slightly.

Betty talked as Eric placed his left hand gently on her back while continuing to clasp her right hand in his. He took a step forward with his left foot and then moved his right foot forward, signaling Betty to move backward. You could see him focus on feeling the music and counting as he led Betty around the dance floor.

"Impressive. You remembered. Class, Eric's doing great. Just like he showed you, leaders start with their left foot, and the followers are going to start with their right. We're going to have two walking steps forward for the leaders and two walking steps back for the followers. What you can't see is that Eric is gently pushing his hand against my back, guiding our direction."

She made eye contact with Eric and continued her instruction. "Don't worry if you don't remember the steps. Everyone here is just learning and hopefully having fun. Let your bodies feel the music and listen closely as I guide you through the steps. Eric and I will do one more pass around the room. Pay particular attention to our feet and how Eric moves his hand against mine. It's a very gentle push in the direction he wants us to travel. If he wants to go back, it's a light grip on my hand and an even lighter pull against my back. It's a slow, slow count. Then we're going to kick it up a bit with a step to the side for a quick, quick count."

Jim whispered in my ear, "It's a turtle, turtle count, then a quick rabbit, rabbit count."

My laugh was more like a loud snort. I put my hand over my mouth, embarrassed.

Betty smiled at us as she moved effortlessly, gliding across the dance floor over to Jess where she gave Eric a slight curtsey before releasing him to her. "Everyone join in."

Jim smiled as he extended his hand. "May I have this dance?"

"Of course." I moved my hips swiftly from side to side to let my sassy skirt flare around me. Jim laughed as he looked down at my high heels. "I told you to put on the steel-toe boots. It's like you haven't met me. Those toes are in serious danger."

I playfully jabbed his chest with my finger. "My toes trust those size 11 boats for shoes." I put my hand in his and moved into his arms. We fox-trotted across the room, following Betty's instructions of "slow, slow, quick, quick." We stumbled and laughed.

"Turtle, turtle, rabbit, rabbit," Jim murmured as he caught the rhythm of Betty's count. "Thank you for signing us up for lessons. At first I was in Eric's camp. I'd rather shove a hot poker in my eye than dance. But after the first few lessons, I'll have to admit I started to love it. I appreciate how you keep things fun and exciting. However, I'm really glad we're past the cooking lesson stage. I'm sure you noticed I've gained ten pounds."

"You're welcome." I patted his stomach. "I didn't notice. You wear it well. Thanks for being such a good sport." I laughed. "Luckily for you, with this stage, you're guaranteed to burn off those pounds."

"Speaking of stages, I know you're trying to keep things from being boring after we retired, but I'd like to put a pause on whatever idea is spinning around in your head for our next adventure. I need to catch my breath and figure out what our new normal is going to be. You okay with that?"

"I'm more than okay with that. It makes sense. Do you want this to be our last class? I don't mind."

"No, I really am enjoying this. I just want a little break before our next adventure."

"You've got it."

I followed his lead, matching his steps. With each circle around the room, our muscles awakened; the rhythm was like oil for our old joints. Jim's hand tightened around mine, his grip steady and reassuring.

We stumbled again. His feet were shuffling, and I tried to hold back the tears. The doctor warned about this symptom. Until this dance, I hadn't noticed. He didn't seem to be bothered by it. He laughed, paused for a beat to get back in sync, and continued when he felt the rhythm.

It was good to see him relax and enjoy himself. This past year, he'd gone into a deep depression. We both did, if I was honest. The diagnosis hit us like a high-speed train, even though deep down I knew something was wrong. He had just turned 65 when he started having a hard time focusing. I just thought he was overworked and needed to retire. I never dreamed it was dementia. I knew there would be a point when he wouldn't remember any of this, and my heart filled with grief.

I looked into his eyes and gave my best smile. "There's something about music that makes me feel alive," I confessed. I'd barely registered the soft smile playing on his lips when he suddenly dipped me, causing me to burst into laughter. "Quit horsing around. We're going to get kicked out of class!"

Jim grinned. "I just love dipping. When do you think we'll learn it?"

"I believe dipping is a part of salsa. We can choose it for our graduation dance in a few weeks, and you can dip away to your heart's content."

Jim's eyes sparkled with excitement. "So, we get to have a senior prom together, after all. Get it?" he joked.

"Yes. We're seniors having a senior prom. You're a very funny man."

Betty reprimanded us. "All right, you two. Keep the shenanigans down to a low roar."

I tried to stifle my amusement but couldn't help but burst into laughter again. "Oh, my goodness. I told you that you're going to get us kicked out of class!"

Jim pulled me close and kissed the top of my head. "Turtle, turtle, rabbit, rabbit," he repeated.

I looked into his eyes. "I love dancing and being in your arms."

"Me, too." He looked around. "Speaking of prom, I feel like I'm in my old high school auditorium dancing with my best gal. How about we sneak out back and neck?"

I smacked his shoulder and giggled. "I was a good girl in high school. But that sounds like a lovely way to end the evening. Wouldn't it be funny if security caught us? We could act like we're scared they're going to tell our parents. I could grab your hand, and we could pretend to make a run for it."

"You? Ms. Compliance, going against the rules? I don't see it." Jim leaned in and nuzzled my neck before spinning me and adding a slight dip.

"Jim, you're incorrigible."

Just like the past few weeks, the hour flew. Betty turned down the volume: her signal our lesson had ended. "Great job, guys! I can tell you've been practicing. Next week, we're going to two-step. If you have cowboy boots and a hat, feel free to dress the part."

My stomach felt like a brick had landed. The weight of knowing there'd be a day when we wouldn't be able to continue settled in my chest, making it hard to breathe. I pushed back the thoughts of being back in reality and instead held on to the joy of this moment with hope. I was determined to hold on to a sense of normalcy until dementia robbed us of everything we held dear. We were still dancing. And for now, that was enough.

I grabbed my purse and turned to Jim when Jess and Eric walked over. Jess gave me a side hug and Eric shook Jim's hand. Besides Betty, they were the only ones we'd shared Jim's condition with. "How are you guys doing?" she asked.

"We're good. Thanks. We're about to head to dinner. Are you guys free to join us?"

"I'm sorry, we can't. We've got to pick up the grand-kids. They're spending the weekend."

Jim laughed. "Again? That's the third weekend in a row. Before you know it, they're going to move in."

Eric held up his hands. "Don't even think it. I love those little curtain climbers, but I'm exhausted the first few hours and about half dead when we bring them back."

Jess nodded. "The kids are a handful. It's not forever. My daughter signed up for a couples' workshop to salvage their marriage. I think the program lasts a few more weeks. At least I hope so. I promise we'll be at game night next month and we can catch up."

"I'm glad they are working on their marriage. I know how much they loved each other and the kids. I'll hold you to game night. I'm really looking forward to it," Jim said.

"Ditto." Jess said.

Chapter 2 Jill

After a long day of prepping, game night was finally underway. Our monthly poker gathering was just what we needed. Tonight was the perfect chance to unwind and think about something other than Jim's declining memory.

I opened my phone's settings and connected it to a small Bluetooth speaker attached to the underside of the kitchen cabinet. With a tap on "play," soft jazz melodies by Miles Davis floated from the speaker, dancing in the air. My shoulders relaxed and moved to the soothing rhythm. I made my way down the kitchen counter and piled four dishes high with crispy chips and my homemade mango salsa. After arranging miniature chocolate chip cookies in a circle around the snacks, I put the plates on a tray and set it on the center of the kitchen table and sat next to Jim. "Fresh from the oven. Dig in."

Eric waved his hand. "Ladies first."

Jess grabbed her plate and took in an exaggerated inhale. "I don't know what I love more, that sweet chocolaty smell, the warmth, or the taste." She popped a cookie in her mouth and rolled her eyes back. "I take that back. It's the taste. It's definitely the taste. Jill, I'm not lying. When you told me you were baking—my mouth's been watering all day!"

I laughed. "I have a container wrapped and ready for you to take home."

She clapped. "You're the best bestie."

Eric grabbed a chip and took a huge scoop of salsa, then dramatically lowered it into his mouth. "Here comes delicious." He mirrored Jess' eye roll and, with his mouth still full, said, "Please tell me you packed us a container of the salsa."

"I didn't, but I will. There's plenty left in the fridge."

He picked up another chip. "You should sell it at the farmers' market. I mean, really, you'd be set for life."

I laughed. "I think I'll just enjoy my golden years making it for friends and family. Thanks for the endorsement and encouragement, though."

Jess shuffled and dealt the hands like a seasoned dealer.

Eric gathered his and smiled as he placed them against his chest. He had the worst poker face.

Jess adjusted her tennis visor. "Game on." She looked at Eric. "I love you, babe, but tonight, I'm taking all your money."

He laughed. "According to the five boxes delivered today, you already do."

She patted his back. "Well, then, I'm taking the rest."

Eric laughed.

Jim pointed to the deck of cards next to Jess. "Don't you need another deck of cards?"

Jess held up the deck. "For poker?"

"Babe, I think you are thinking of canasta. We haven't played that in years."

Jim looked at his cards. "I guess I'm in for five bucks then."

Eric gave a whistle. "That must be some hand. I thought we were sticking to Penny Ante."

"I meant five pennies."

Jess and I took out our canvas bags of pennies and filled the four fruit cup bowls around the table. She placed one in front of her and one in front of Eric and I did the same for Jim and I.

Jess turned her attention to Jim. "Saving a good card for later?"

"What?"

She pointed to his shirt. "The card in your shirt pocket. Is that for a magic show later or are you saving it for a big win?"

Jim pulled out the card from his pocket. "It must have slid down when I was holding the cards." The concern on his face shifted to a smile as he tried to deflect from the awkward moment. "Good catch, pocket!"

Jess and Eric exchange glances as I pushed down the memory of his wallet in the refrigerator last week.

"That was a good catch!" I agreed.

Jim and Jess' bantering gave me just enough time to grab a pitcher of margaritas from the counter. As I poured drinks for everyone but Jim, I couldn't help but notice Eric's eyebrows raise at Jim's water glass.

"You skipping Jill's Famous Marg, brother?"

"I'm skipping the hard stuff. I just have a bit of wine now and again. Trying not to mix alcohol and medicine too much. I don't want to melt my liver."

"Do you want some lemonade in a margarita glass so you won't feel left out?" he asked.

"No. Thanks. I've had to slow down over the past few years, anyway. It's not a bad thing. I'm not uncomfortable if you're not."

Eric held up his glass and toasted everyone. "To game night and healthy livers. I'll work on mine tomorrow if that's okay?" He took a sip.

Jess took a generous sip. "These are too delicious to pass up. I'll join you tomorrow, babe."

"Of course. I'll have to stick with one marg. I don't want to kill too many brain cells. I'm having trouble with the old memory these days, too."

Jess poked Eric in the arm. "Really, sweetie pie?"

"What?" His head snapped towards Jim. "Jeez, not like yours. I mean, no comparison."

Jess put her hand on Eric's. "You're making it worse."

Eric hung his head slightly. He raised his eyes to Jim. "I didn't mean to be insensitive."

Jim's laugh diffused the tension. "Don't worry, brother. I think this nasty memory thing's going to get us all one day. I've already forgotten the comment. Can we play cards before I forget how?"

Eric and Jess laughed and nodded.

I sat down and changed the subject. "Let's do this. I'm feeling lucky tonight. Mama needs a new pair of shoes."

We all laughed. At that moment, surrounded by good friends, I knew we could handle the challenges dementia had in store for us.

Chapter 3 Jim

I loved working in the garden. Over the years we filled it with trees, shrubs, and plants of all shapes and sizes, but then came the weeds. They sprouted in every nook and cranny. I actually liked the ones that had the daisy-like flowers. When I became principal of our local high school, weed pulling took a backseat. I had the bright idea of adding rock beds for low maintenance. That turned out to be the worst decision when the goat head weeds poked through. They were the fastest growing buggers I'd ever seen, with deep roots that held on for dear life.

I'd spent the first part of my morning pulling out the easier chickweed and shallow-rooted clover. My bucket was full. I looked around, wiping sweat off my brow, trying to decide if I was going to take a break or tackle some more. The sun was getting higher in the sky and I didn't want to burn, so I made my way to the shaded rock bed to knock it out.

Pulling weeds wasn't on the schedule, but I needed to do something physical to get out of my head. When I woke up this morning, I couldn't stop playing the loop of everyone's faces last night when I blundered. I thought I'd been better at hiding my deterioration, but their shifting eyes proved I wasn't as successful as I thought. Maybe the first year, but not now.

Initially, it was easy to disguise my slipping memory from Jill, friends and coworkers. I knew I had trouble finding words but no one else suspected. I had an extensive vocabulary. When the word I wanted didn't surface, I plucked a different one with barely a pause. But over time, words were harder to grab, much like the stubborn weeds were harder to pull. The delays to substitute words became longer and more noticeable.

I continued to pull weeds from the rocks, but the physical exertion and heat weren't enough to distract me from the realization that it was becoming more challenging to hide my decline. I tugged at a stubborn dandelion. It snapped, leaving the root behind. I sat back, frustrated. I wanted more than anything to douse the entire rock bed with weed kill, but since the diagnosis, we were full-on organic. Another change that could possibly help my mental state.

I thought about Jill and everything she had done to make sure we stayed healthy. Jill was my rock. When she first complained about my forgetting to run errands on the way home, or losing my keys or sunglasses, I turned on her and called her a nag. She wasn't really nagging, and not really complaining. She was concerned that I was working too hard. Jill wanted me to slow down and retire. When I attacked her, I wasn't ready to tell her something was wrong. Maybe it was my pride that made me deny something was happening. In either case, I chose to hurt her in order to protect me, to protect us from the painful truth. The truth I already knew.

For several months before Jill's observations, I'd been showing up to the wrong meetings at work or missing meetings entirely. I blamed it on my electronic calendar. No one questioned it at first, then everyone shifted uncomfortably in their seats when the occurrences became more frequent.

I should have reached out to my doctor, or at least Jill, when it got even worse. Like when I had trouble understanding instructions in meetings. When I kept asking my peers to repeat themselves. I told them I was hard of hearing. I left so many meetings feeling like I had a handle on the next steps, but when I'd discuss it with someone as a follow up, I'd realize I was completely off base. Yes, I knew something wasn't right well before Jill started questioning my forgetfulness.

The diagnosis took almost a full year after I finally reached out. At first my doctor told me I had high blood pressure. He assured me hypertension caused my forgetfulness and brain fog. Six months later, my blood pressure was under control, but the fog never cleared. In fact, it deepened. I forgot the names of students. I'd always prided myself on knowing not only their names, but enough personal details to hold a quick conversation. Then I couldn't handle people talking over each other at meetings. I knew it was time to retire when I kept asking, "What do you think?" I was the Principal, I had to be comfortable making final decisions.

Soon after that, everything felt like sensory overload. Even the clanking of dishes at restaurants rattled my nerves. I finally consulted a neurologist, and he confirmed the diagnosis. He was honest and direct. I'll never forget his warning not to give in to fear. He told me damage to the brain affects everyone differently and to stay away from movies about dementia. They only show the moment of diagnosis and jump to a not-so-pleasant end stage in a two-hour period.

He told me there can be a decade or more of living after the diagnosis and although it wouldn't be an easy journey, I could still experience joy and happiness. His advice was for Jill and me to join support groups, make friends, exercise, go for walks, and follow a clean diet. The point being we would *live* with dementia. We had to stay active, stay engaged and keep my mind challenged. I had to celebrate the wins. Although I might not grab a word as easily as I could a few years ago, and I might ask the same questions over and over, I could still take a car engine apart. I could still draw a clock.

I looked over at the rose garden and grinned as I grabbed my pocket snips. I had to show Jill my gratitude and how much I loved her. The start to this bouquet was a few creamy yellow blooms with soft pink edges from the peace rose bush. Their fruity scent was her favorite. Then I cut five velvety red roses to encircle the softer pinks. Their scent was much stronger, like a heady perfume. I added three white roses to the middle bundle and made my way to the kitchen for a vase.

Chapter 4 Jill

I loved the aroma of baked tomato sauce and melted cheese. My masterpiece was ready. I placed a hefty portion of lasagna on both plates and added two pieces of garlic bread before the heat seared my fingertips. I sank into the chair across from Jim with a heavy sigh, eyeing the half-empty wine bottle.

I was looking forward to dinner, but just wanted one minute of peace before the endless loop started again.

"I can't remember if I have any meetings in the morning," Jim said, moving the lasagna around with his fork.

And here we go. "No babe, you're retired." We'd had this exact exchange at least a dozen times in the past week.

Jim frowned. "I just hang out here while you're at work? That's boring. Did you have a full day of kids shooting spit balls?"

"Don't be an old coot. You know the students are at risk and come from troubled homes. They're not bad kids. And no, all that's behind me. I'm retired."

"Must be nice. I had back-to-back meetings approving budgets for all the departments. All went well. I shot down a few, but approved most."

I poured another glass and savored a long sip. "This red pairs well with the meal. Do you like the lasagna? It's your mother's recipe."

He shook his head and glanced at my glass. "Is that a new bottle? What kind is it?"

I tightened my grip, breathing slowly to suppress my rising frustration. "It's the same cabernet we opened last night."

He set his fork down with a hard clank. "I don't think it goes with the lasagna at all. I don't think anything would go with it."

He knew I'd spent all afternoon cooking. I clenched my jaw to stop the heated response threatening to burst out. *Let it go, Jill. Just let it go. Breathe.* "You don't like it? It's always been your favorite. I didn't deviate from the recipe at all."

"It's too heavy. Why didn't you make tomato soup and grilled cheese? Those are my favorite."

Since when? That was the first time he'd ever told me tomato soup and grilled cheese were his favorite. I took a long sip of wine and suppressed the urge to scream, *"I'll make your precious tomato soup tomorrow."* Instead, I said, "I'll make that tomorrow, babe."

Jim's jaw relaxed. "Did you have a busy day? Did your students behave?"

The words stuck in my throat. *I'm retired,* I wanted to shout. *We're both retired, you have dementia!* Instead, I swallowed hard. "All that's behind me. I'm retired."

Jim smirked. "Must be nice. My eyeballs are bloodshot from crunching numbers all day."

I didn't correct him this time. Maybe in his mind he had been a principal again—successful, healthy, happy, admired by the staff, respected by the students. I reached across the table and squeezed his hand. "That's nice, dear."

We finished dinner in silence. He ate his garlic bread and continued to play with his food.

Jim stood as I cleared the dishes. "I've got an early meeting tomorrow and better get to bed."

Entering his reality once more, I responded, "Alright. Sleep tight. I'll join you after I finish cleaning up."

He headed to the bathroom to brush his teeth. I finished the last of my wine and let it rest on my tongue, resolving to be more patient tomorrow after a good night's sleep.

The wine relaxed me and crumbled my walls. I knew I needed to find healthier ways to relax, but for tonight I rested my head on my arms and let the sobs wrack my body. A few weeks ago, we found out Jim's MoCA test used to detect cognitive decline and early signs of dementia came back with a lower score. I actually didn't need for him to take the test to know that, but I wanted to see how much he had declined. I loved this man with all of my heart, but I was ashamed to admit the past few months of the same stories and repeated questions were wearing me down. There were still times my old Jim was there. Today was not one of them.

None of this was his fault, and I know he'd be more patient and forgiving with me if the roles were reversed. It was a good cry and a cathartic release. I rinsed out my wine glass, loaded the dishwasher and headed to bed. The night-stand lamp illuminated the most beautiful arrangement of roses from our garden, and I broke down crying all over again. I turned off the light and climbed in bed. Jim's light snores filled the room. I snuggled over to him and held him tight.

Chapter 5 Jim

I stared at the dark circles around my eyes in the bathroom mirror, then traced my finger across the toothbrush in my hand. The bristles were dry. I ran my tongue across the front of my teeth just to double check. *I could've sworn I'd brushed my teeth a few minutes ago.* Jill, calling me to the kitchen, pulled me out of my thoughts.

"Jim, your oatmeal is ready. Get in here before it gets cold."

"Coming!" When I walked into the kitchen, the smell of coffee and cinnamon oatmeal made my stomach growl. "Babe, did you notice anything strange about my toothbrush this morning?"

She put her hands on her hips. "That's an odd question. I don't make a habit of inspecting your toothbrush. Why?"

"I'm almost certain I brushed my teeth earlier, but now I'm not so sure."

"Are you sure you didn't just get distracted and thought you brushed your teeth? Maybe your toothbrush dried quicker than you thought."

"You're probably right. Brushing my teeth is such an autopilot thing to do. I bet I just got distracted. I'm over analyzing everything I do, looking for signs I'm getting worse."

Jill pulled the kitchen chair out for me. "Nothing to fret over. Now sit down and eat some oatmeal. You need to keep your strength up. I noticed you've been eating less and less. Your clothes are hanging on you."

"I can't eat. I'll be late for work," I protested.

"Honey, you're retired," Jill sighed.

Just when I was comforted by her not being concerned about my toothbrush, she throws me with the "retired" comment.

She furrowed her brow and frowned as I took her hand. "Retired? What are you talking about?" To support the fact that I was off to work, I wiggled my tie. "Then why am I wearing this darn thing?" I grumbled.

Jill straightened it with expertise. "Remember when you got ready this morning? You thought you were interviewing a new teacher?"

I barely heard her. Her voice seemed distant. I leaned in and tried to focus.

She patted my tie. Her signal it was perfection. "I told you to keep it on. You looked so handsome."

I looked down at her forced smile. She looked so tired. "Of course I don't remember. I just told you I have to feel my toothbrush five minutes after walking out of the bathroom to see if it is wet, because I can't even remember if I brushed my dang teeth." It wasn't fair to snap at her. It was me and my forgetfulness I was mad at.

She stepped back. "Do you think it's time to go to the memory care center the doctor told us about?"

"No! I'm not like them. Maybe the retirement thing was just a pattern of getting ready. You just said I was distracted. It doesn't mean I've gotten worse. I took too long to check my toothbrush; that's what you said. I remember that."

Her eyes softened as she smiled. "How about you give me a kiss, and I'll let you know if they're brushed?"

I pressed my lips against hers, then pulled back. "Did I pass?"

She playfully pushed me away while pinching her nose and fanning the air. "Sorry, babe. Epic fail. Serious morning breath," she teased. Her laughter triggered a vivid image of us laughing at my retirement party. I was retired!

I know so many people look forward to retiring. I wasn't one of them. It made me feel like I'd stopped contributing. I felt irrelevant. Helping Jill volunteer and joining her on all her new hobbies made a difference. I can't believe such a milestone fell into the dark hole of my stupid Swiss cheese of a brain. What was next?

I reached for my phone, hoping to make amends. "I remember now. You wore that sassy skirt of yours for my retirement party. We were the last ones on the dance floor. For going above and beyond your marriage vows with the sniff test, let's dance to our song," I said, scrolling through my playlist, stopping in confusion. *Shit, I can't remember our song.* "Babe, I'm sorry. What's our song?" I asked sheepishly, embarrassed at my second bout of forgetfulness. I hoped she wasn't keeping score. Two in a row and we hadn't even sat down for breakfast.

Jill smiled, took my phone, found our song and hit "play." As the melody filled the room, I held out my hand to her. "May I have this dance? No fancy moves, just a slow dance with you in my arms." I prayed I'd never forget this moment. Well, except for the part where I forgot to brush my teeth.

Laughing, Jill reached for my hand. Holding her close, I softly kissed the top of her head as she nestled into my shoulder.

I raised her chin and gazed into her eyes. "I may not remember everything, but I promise you, somehow a part of me will still cherish this moment."

She gave me a gentle kiss and wiped a tear from her eye.

Chapter 6 Jill

Jess turned on her blinker and made a left down Elm Street.

I shifted in my seat. "I'm sorry you keep having to do this. You're a lifesaver."

"It's only been a few times. Don't worry about it. I'm here for you. Did you track him on the app again?"

"No. I thought he was at the store. I gave them my number last time. They called me as soon as they saw his car in the driveway."

I pointed toward the windshield. "There he is."

She nodded. "I see him on the porch."

Jess pulled into the driveway behind Jim's car. "I'll stay here until I get the all-clear signal."

I nodded and reached for the door handle. "Thank you. I'll call you when we get home."

"Jill, it's going to be okay. Take a deep breath."

I took a few shaky breaths, jumped out, and slammed the door behind me. I made my way over to the porch of our old one-story home, my heart pounding against my chest. Jim sitting with his head in his hands had no idea we were here. Mike and Angela, the young couple that bought the house a few years ago, stood in front of him. Mike's arm wrapped around her. They stepped back when they saw me.

"I'm so sorry this keeps happening," I apologized to the couple. "Thank you for calling me."

Angela's eyes brimmed with tears. "We went through something like this with my grandmother. Just keep him safe."

Her words stung. It was my job to keep him safe, and I was failing miserably. "I will. This won't happen again. I promise."

Jim stood up as I approached him, taking his hand in mine. I tried to keep my voice steady. "Jim, let's go home, babe."

He tried to pull his hand back. "This is my home. I don't know why these people are here. They won't let me in."

I met his eyes. "Jim, we haven't lived here in twenty years," I pointed towards the couple. "This is Mike and Angela's home now."

Jim stopped resisting. His shoulders slumped. "This isn't our home?"

"It was, just not anymore." I put my arm around his shoulder and directed him to our car. "Let me show you our new home. You're going to love it."

As we walked past the owners, I gave them an apologetic smile. "Thank you."

They returned sympathetic nods.

Jim looked back at the house, confused.

I pressed on his shoulder to follow. "It's okay, babe. I'm here."

We made our way to the car, and I helped him into the passenger seat. I reached for the seatbelt.

He pushed my hand away. "You don't have to buckle me. I'm not a child."

"I'm sorry. I wasn't thinking."

I got into the driver's side and leaned back against the headrest. My hands were shaking. I needed a moment to regain my composure and let my heart stop pounding. "Everything's okay. I'll make us a nice dinner when we get home."

Jim turned and looked out his window, not responding.

I gave Jess a thumbs up and she backed out of the driveway.

I patted Jim's leg. "Let's get you home."

As I pulled out of the driveway, I thought about my promise to never let it happen again. The only way I could keep it was to take the keys from Jim. A conversation I knew was inevitable, but didn't think it would be happening this soon.

Chapter 7 Jim

I clutched the keys to our SUV as I stepped onto the driveway. My hand gripped the door handle, but I couldn't seem to lift it. It wasn't stuck; I was. My feet were like lead bolting me to the floor. I wanted to drive more than anything, but I also didn't, because I knew it would be the last time I would be behind the wheel. Last night was the first time Jill drew the line with no compromise. I recognized our home as soon as we pulled in. I tried to explain, I just got confused. I knew we didn't live on Elm Street anymore. She wasn't hearing it and threatened to run my license through the shredder if I didn't willingly surrender it to her.

I took a deep breath, opened the door, and slid into the driver's seat. I pulled the door closed, leaned back, and inhaled the smell of leather. The steering wheel felt warm from the sun as I moved it like I did when I was eight, making vroom-vroom noises, pretending to drive while Dad filled up the gas tank. I knew I could talk Dad into letting me drive as soon as I was tall enough to reach the pedals. Of course, he didn't let me until I could get my driver's permit. Now, more than a few decades later, my aging hands were just as barred from driving as those tiny ones.

At dinner when I agreed to let Jill take on the role as family driver, I didn't expect the simple things, like the sun warming my face through the windshield or the sound of the key as I put it in the ignition, would trigger such a profound feeling of loss. I thought about our road trips over the years. I couldn't remember where we went for most, but I knew we both loved the open road and the joy of new experiences.

When the engine roared to life, I pounded the steering wheel. Damn this fog creeping into every crevice of my brain. It was bad enough my life with Jill was on the edge of being erased. I never thought it would rob me of my identity as well. This thought surprised me because, until that moment, I didn't realize being the family driver was even a part of my identity.

I made a left out of our driveway. A pang in my heart replaced the usual feeling of exhilaration at being behind the wheel. I was about to be a prisoner in my own home. I had enough sense to know that wasn't true. Jill would take me anywhere I needed to go, and I could call a ride share if needed. It was nevertheless devastating to think this would be my last time behind the wheel. Handing over the key to Jill would be like handing over a part of myself, and I didn't have many parts to spare.

I headed to the grocery store to prove my abilities weren't that far gone. Maybe she'd let me drive a bit longer. If not, I couldn't let a circle in the neighborhood be my last experience behind the wheel. I took the side streets to get Jill some flowers. She'd be mad, but fingers crossed, the flowers and my safe return would lessen her fears.

As I eased onto the road, the hum of the engine wrapped around me like a hug. With each passing mile, I tightened my grip on the wheel, determined to hold on to this fleeting moment of freedom. I lowered the window and let the wind flow over my hand as I dangled my arm. I focused on the drive, determined to take in the beauty of the trees as the sunlight bounced off the leaves, turning the roadside into a priceless painting.

Within a few miles, I couldn't recognize the street names or what I was certain were familiar landmarks, but I couldn't place them in the context of where I was. With trembling hands, I clutched the steering wheel and swallowed hard, trying to steady my breathing. I fought against panicking, but my pulse quickened in defiance. My heart pounded. I strained to recall the turns that would lead me to the store. They were as out of reach as the words on the tip of my tongue that more and more I couldn't quite articulate. Every mile of unfamiliar road brought beads of sweat to my forehead. The world was closing in. My ears rang from the blood pressure pounding through my veins. I pulled over and looked at the cross streets and thought about calling Jill to come get me. It was the last thing I wanted to do but my confidence was shattered, and I was in no shape to drive. A light emanated from the navigation system. Could I trust it? Was the home address entered correctly? I took a few deep breaths. *Get a hold of yourself, man; of course it is.* I selected "home."

I relied on the navigator to guide me. "In 500 feet, turn left onto Main Street." The unit's voice was calm and comforting. Her instructions were breadcrumbs, leading me back to Jill.

I took a deep breath and gave an audible "thank you" every time that sweet voice told me to turn. My death grip on the wheel loosened as the tension drained away. I knew I'd make it back safely, despite the unfamiliar houses lining my path.

As I turned into my development, my awareness came flooding back. My heartbeat returned to normal, as did my breathing. Once I turned on our street, the homes became more familiar. First, I recognized our recreation center and tennis courts, then I recognized Bob and Jane's ugly yellow house. I remembered countless walks with Jill and our old pups.

Despite having returned safely, my nerves buzzed like bees as I pulled into our driveway. Jill was right to ask for my keys. Entering through the front door, I found her pacing as she waited anxiously for my return. Her worried expression softened as I approached, but quickly vanished when she met my eyes.

Even though I knew she was right, I gripped the cold metal keys in my hand, not wanting to release them. What was almost weightless in my hand seemed to pull down on my shoulders. My body fought what my mind knew was inevitable. I opened my palm and handed her my independence, my manhood. Jill took the keys and hugged me. "I was so worried. I'm sorry I betrayed your privacy, but I activated the vehicle's locator. Were you headed to the store?"

I nodded. "I wanted to bring you some flowers. But I can't even do that. Thank heavens for technology or I'd still be driving around in circles. You're right, hon, it's time." My heart felt like I'd been kicked in the chest. I knew with that reaction, I'd change my mind and wanted to make the fight she'd be having easier. "Please promise me no matter how hard I insist, you won't hand them back."

Tears welled up in Jill's eyes as she stared at the keys. "I promise, Jim. No matter what happens, I won't let you drive."

She took my hand and led me into our living room. Much like the windshield, the warm glow of afternoon filled the room and raised the temperature a few degrees. We collapsed on our old leather couch and, without a word, leaned back and closed our eyes. She held my hand tight. The silence held space, offering understanding and empathy. I squeezed her hand with a surge of gratitude for her allowing me to process my feelings in silence until I was ready to share.

"Hon, I got lost." My voice shook. "It's not the first time. It's been happening for months, but the system's always gotten me where I needed to go. Until today, I had more familiar than unfamiliar parts of the drive. Today, I was driving blind all the way home. I had to trust the unit 100%. My memory's worse."

"I'm so sorry, babe. Are you okay if we go check out the memory care center Dr. Garza told us about? It's near the house. He said they can help us develop strategies as you progress."

"I'm ready."

"I love you." Her eyes glistened as she fought back tears.

"I love you too, hon. I just feel like we've shifted from a husband-wife partnership to a parent-child relationship. You tell me when to take my meds, when my appointments are. You keep track of everything I can't remember. Driving was the one thing I felt control over. I could decide to turn left or right. I could decide where to go and how to get there."

"I'm sorry I've turned into a nag about your meds."

"You're not nagging, hon. It's the fact that you have to do it. Not that you are. You see the distinction, right?"

"I do. I don't mind, but I totally get it. Let's ask the support group if there're ways to keep you independent."

"Thanks, babe." I closed my eyes, the weight in my chest lifting slightly, as I rested my head on her soft, warm shoulders, and surrendered to the vulnerability of my progression.

Chapter 8 Jill

I glanced nervously at Jim as we walked through the community center doors. This was our first time attending a dementia support group, and neither of us knew quite what to expect. Jim's tight grip on my hand told me he was just as nervous. As we took our seats among the circle of chairs, we exchanged smiles and nods with a few others who all seemed to notice our apprehension and returned understanding nods. Soft, calming classical music played from a small speaker in the corner, instantly soothing my rattled nerves.

A tall woman in her thirties sat across from us. "Hello everyone. Most of you already know me. For the benefit of the new faces in the group, I'm Janet, your facilitator."

I felt the tension leave Jim's hand. Her warmth put us at ease.

Janet gazed at us. "I see we have two new guests tonight. Would you like to introduce yourselves?"

Jim nodded for me to go first. "I'm Jill Bish." I bumped my shoulder against Jim's. "I'm Jim's wife and I guess down the road, caregiver. He was diagnosed last year with dementia. Life is becoming challenging. We've done a lot of research, but I... I mean, we felt like we needed help navigating the waters. His doctor suggested this group."

"As introduced by my lovely wife, I'm Jim and, if things keep going this quickly, soon-to-be her patient, I guess. Not sure what I'm called—care receiver?"

Janet smiled. "Welcome, Jill and Jim. This program is more about social connection than medical, although we have medical guest speakers. While caregiver is the common term and not wrong, there has been a shift to care partner. Mentally, the term caregiver can feel like a solo responsibility. That as a caregiver, *you* must meet all needs.

Without help, caregivers can end up pouring all of their energy into helping the person they love while possibly neglecting themselves. Partners work together. The term care partner acknowledges caregiving is not a solitary task but a joint effort. Multiple people, including family, friends, support groups, and professionals, can be part of this partnership. The focus is on finding solutions that enhance the quality of life for the person with dementia. Here we call everyone participants."

"I love that. As a teacher, I couldn't agree more. The language we use matters." I said.

Janet nodded. "Thanks, Jill. I'm glad you took your doctor's advice. Self-care and support are critical. Jim, I can't make any promises, but I think we can help teach you techniques that might make things feel less like you're on a fast roller-coaster. You're in good company," Janet assured us. "The participants have all been in your shoes. Everyone's in a different place on the journey, but we're all on it together and here to support you and share our experiences. It's not an easy journey, but this group's goal is to help make it a little lighter and hopefully easier. Jill, I'm glad to hear you're doing research. One of the most critical components of acceptance is to educate yourself about dementia—its stages, symptoms, and how it affects you as a care partner and Jim's cognitive abilities."

"Thank you. We appreciate everyone's help in figuring this out." I smiled slightly.

"That's why we're here." She gave us a reassuring smile. "I'm not sure if you went online about the program, but it's a weekly meeting in a four-hour block. We start off together with hellos and a fun activity like puzzles. About thirty minutes into the shared activity, the care partners move to a separate room to share experiences and learnings from what worked and didn't work since the last session. The participant continues to work on the tasks and can ask questions or share concerns with the program director or join in light exercises. Then everyone comes together to finish the task. This allows care partners to have a safe space to talk freely and learn from each other. We end the day with a nice catered lunch donated by a local nursing home. It's usually gourmet sandwiches and hearty soups. Today we are going to skip the activity as we have a special lesson. I'm not only excited to introduce the topic, but I'm also thrilled to share that it's going to be presented by none other than our favorite eldercare nurse, Vicky Taylor."

A woman two chairs from Janet stood and took a bow. Everyone clapped. "Hello, I'm Vicky and I'm going to share how the power of music can help you along your journey."

I looked at Jim, seeing a glimmer of interest light up his eyes. His smile faded at Vicky's next comment. "But first, why don't the care partners make their way to room 2B for about a half hour, and everyone else stay and I can answer questions?"

Jim looked at me, hesitant to split up. I kissed his cheek. "I know we tell each other everything. It might be good to have someone else to talk to who knows what you're going through." It had to be good for him. I know for me, I was really looking forward to being able to talk to people who knew what I was going through.

He nodded.

"I'll be back before you know it."

I followed Janet to the room.

She pointed towards a table on the far wall when we entered. "There are a few recommended books and a list of online resources on the table that others in the group found helpful. Help yourself to whatever resonates with you. Everyone's journey is unique."

We took our seats in another circle of chairs.

An older gentleman sat next to me and chimed in, "You couldn't be more right, Janet. Understanding the progression of the disease is crucial." He turned to me. "I'd like to point out while the journeys aren't identical, there are patterns. Memory loss might be the focus now because it's the first symptom, but as time goes on, your Jim may have trouble with communication, possibly mood swings, and even difficulty completing tasks he did with his eyes closed and one arm tied behind his back. Almost every day has its challenges, but praise be, there are victories as well. Celebrate the wins. There are no wins too small. Focus on what you can do now and tuck and roll as needed."

I pulled a tissue out from my purse and dabbed at the edges of my eye. I never thought to focus on the wins. Everything we lost and were going to lose was all I could see. "That's helpful. Thank you."

Janet nodded. "Good call-outs, William. Jill, it's important to remember that should Jim's actions or behaviors change, they're a result of the disease, not a result of how you're caring for him or his love for you. Try not to take things personally. Jim's not intentionally forgetting your birthday or getting frustrated easily. It's the disease. Patience is powerful. Avoid saying 'You remember', as it can be exasperating and triggering, as clearly, he can't remember. Try your best to maintain your cool. You'll both have good days, bad days and some really tough days. Take care of yourself and find healthy outlets for your own emotions. It's perfectly okay to feel overwhelmed. Reach out to friends, family, or one of us. Everyone's phone number is on a list on the table."

I cried and rocked in my chair with my hand on my forehead. "I'm doing it all wrong. I say, 'You remember' all day long. One reason we came today is because Jim keeps forgetting he's retired. He was trying to go to work the other day. When I stopped him, I could tell he was confused and thrown off, but then he remembered. So, wasn't it good that I said, 'You remember'?"

Janet touched my hand. "Don't think of it as wrong. Think of it as if there might be a better way to reach Jim without upsetting or contradicting him. In Jim's mind, his reality is as sound as yours. At this early stage, reminders may help trigger a memory, but it's better to get in the practice of not disagreeing. There'll be a point when it causes severe agitation. It's best to join him in his reality if it's safe to do so."

"So, I should have let him go to work? That would have really confused him when someone else was sitting in his old office and everyone asking why he was there."

"Good point. If he tries to leave the house, you can't always follow his reality, but you can agree and distract or redirect. You'll be surprised how quickly he'll relax when you agree. Within minutes, he'll forget what he wanted to do."

"I should have said, 'You won't be late. Let's eat breakfast first'? Or even, 'It's a holiday; the office is closed'?"

"Those are good. Always start with a redirect or distraction. We try not to lie if at all possible. If he's not distracted by breakfast, then the holiday might be a good option."

William raised his hand. "My Sally always asks when her sister is visiting. At first, I kept reminding her that her sister had passed. It was devastating to her. Every day, I made her relive her sister's death. Once I joined this group, I learned to ask her to tell me stories about her sister. I would say, 'It sounds like you really miss her. I miss her, too. What's the thing you like the most about the two of you?' Usually that worked. As a last resort, if she was inconsolable, I'd tell her Julie's coming over for lunch tomorrow. She would smile and say, 'Oh, that's nice.'"

I nodded. "That's so helpful; thank you all. I'll grab a copy of the resources and contact info on my way out. I'm going to need help. Some days, my emotions feel like I just stepped on a roller coaster, and other days, my brain feels like I just stepped off a teacup ride."

Janet nodded. "We'll see if we can't slow the rides down." The rest of the participants took turns sharing their stories and giving me insights into what I might expect in the coming months and years. Hearing their helpful hints on how to handle challenges gave me hope, but did little to lift the weight from the realization that this journey could last a decade or longer.

We made our way back to the original room and returned to our seats. I gave Jim a hug and sat down next to him. "How'd it go?"

"You're right. It helps to share with someone who's been where I am. It's scary to hear where they are, but it helps."

Janet opened her phone, and with a gentle touch, changed the song. A familiar tune filled the room, and I tapped my foot to the rhythm. Jim nudged me, a wide grin spreading across his face as he recognized the melody. It was one of our favorite songs from our early years together.

Vicky clapped. "I see it's working already." She beamed as some of us moved to the music. "The beauty of music is that even when other memories fade, the connection to music often remains intact. It's not only therapeutic;

it provides an emotional release. Why don't we take turns sharing your favorite memories involving music?"

One woman raised her hand. "It's true." Tears rolled down her cheeks as she recounted the power of music. "My father was deep into the fog of dementia and wouldn't even acknowledge any of us when we entered the room." She slapped her leg. "But, boy howdy, put on music from his twenties and he would suddenly light up, sing along, and before we left, he was telling us one story after the other about his youth."

Vicky nodded. "A very common experience. Thanks for sharing. Anyone else? Don't be shy."

Another gentleman raised his hand. "When my wife Christy had difficulty with even the most basic tasks, she became her old self when we played songs from our wedding. I mean, almost her old self. She was animated and with the biggest grin. For those few precious moments, she'd dance like she was young again."

Another woman elbowed her husband and blurted, "When my old coot gets all wadded up, I play his favorite song, and he calms right down!"

Vicky laughed. "Another great example of how music can help. It's very effective at reducing anxiety and agitation. As most of you have discovered, people living with dementia often experience frustration, anxiety, and agitation because of their confusion and irritation with their inability to communicate. Music does indeed calm the beast, as they say. It has a soothing effect that helps keep negative emotions at bay. You'll be happy to know that listening to familiar songs or even joining music therapy classes can reduce agitation levels significantly. It's a combination of rhythm, melody, and repetition that settles the nerves, and improves mood. It's a win-win for the patient and care partner. Besides being a happy pill, music therapy has been shown to improve cognitive function, attention, and overall mental well-being in individuals with dementia. Musical activities encourage the brain to form new neural connections, helping to preserve cognitive abilities for as long as possible."

I squeezed Jim's hand. I was excited our dance class was more than a hobby or a source of entertainment. It had the power to bring back Jim's forgotten memories and even calm him when he felt irritated or cranky, which happened more often these days. Leaving the support group, Jim and I held onto each other a little tighter. I let out an audible sigh of relief. My shoulders felt lighter, we weren't alone.

Chapter 9 Jill

Rocking on the porch in our weathered and creaky wicker chairs, Jim and I watched the leaves scatter in the autumn breeze. We were excited about Vicky's visit and the suggestions she would make to help Jim stay as independent as possible as his condition progressed. I really liked her and was glad when the Memory Café assigned her as our dementia caseworker. She exuded warmth and empathy, and everyone couldn't stop talking about how her advice was so simple, yet life changing.

"Hello, Mr. and Mrs. Bish," Vicky called out as she made her way to the porch.

I jumped up and gave her a big hug. "Please, it's Jill and Jim. Thanks so much for putting us on your rotation."

Jim stood and gave her a firm handshake with a few pumps. "Yes, thank you."

"It's my pleasure. I was happy to discover you're less than a mile from my house. I'm in the neighborhood right before yours."

"No kidding. That's awesome." I opened the screen door and motioned for Jim to enter. Vicky followed. We gathered around the kitchen table. As Vicky settled into the chair, I noticed her looking at my fall setting. I was quite proud of my seasonal decorations and thought she would compliment me as she took it all in.

She turned to Jim. "Jim, getting diagnosed with dementia is most definitely a defining moment, but it doesn't have to define you. It's a part of your life now. With a few adjustments, we can keep you in control of your daily tasks and routines. We just need to monitor changes and adjust accordingly. Have you had any changes in eyesight?"

"Yes, I don't just need readers anymore. My eyesight is definitely deteriorating. It takes more time to focus, and my peripheral vision isn't what it used to be."

I smacked my forehead, realizing I hadn't even thought of his vision being the reason he'd been having a hard time eating or startled easily when I walked up to him. I thought his hearing was off, but maybe he couldn't see me. "He's knocked over the water glass a few times. Sorry, babe, I didn't think about your vision getting worse."

Vicky nodded. "It's something I like to see checked. Jim, I think it might be a good idea to see if your changes warrant a prescription upgrade from readers. Jill, although your setting is beautiful, it's all the same color. There is no contrast which makes it difficult to make out the edges of the plates. Let's see if contrasting colors help. For example, if you have white plates, use a dark placemat. If you have a dark placemat, use a lighter solid color table cloth. This applies to the bathroom, too. It's usually all white. Add some colorful mats and a colored toilet seat to help with the aim, if you know what I mean."

We all laughed.

Vicky made eye contact with Jim. "How about we create a visual schedule of your appointments and medications? Something large enough for you to see with reminders of what meds to take and when. This can help you stay organized, and you can keep some sense of control. We can set up alarms on your phone when it's time to take your meds or leave for an appointment."

Jim's face brightened, and I caught glimpses of the vibrant man he used to be. "I'd like that very much."

She pointed to the cabinets. "A project you can do together is label drawers, cupboards, and rooms with pictures of what's in there. Jim, this will help you locate items around the house on your own. We should place anything that might eventually become a danger above or below eye level. No need for child locks. It can be frustrating. Just don't have a picture on the door or drawer and it will be out of sight, out of mind. For example, take any large carving or butcher knives from the silverware drawer so Jim can make sandwiches and meals with butter knives, reducing the risk of cuts. Jim, these small things will help bring stability and familiarity to your daily routine. I have one more thing I think you will enjoy."

She pulled a book out of her bag and handed it to Jim. He thumbed through it. "I know there are plenty of caregiver or, as we like to call it, care partner resources Jill picked up during her session. This one's for you. That's a book filled with brain exercises and memory games. Keeping your mind stimulated might slow down the progression."

Jim continued to turn the pages. "This means a lot. I hate that I have to rely on Jill for everything. I'd like to hold on to my independence as long as I can. That's why you're assigned to us. Right?"

Vicky smiled. "That's right. My role is to help outside of the support group. Actually, all of us at the agency are part of a tiered system. We can do simple house visits, more detailed medical visits, and, as things progress, we can even move in as part-time or full-time aids. I removed myself from the last tier. It was too hard on my husband and dog."

"I get that. I wouldn't want to be separated from Jill several nights a week while she stayed at someone else's house."

"Yes, it's usually the ones without family who sign up for that last tier. I did weekends for about a year, but even that was too much time away from the family." She laughed. "Depending on the state of a person's marriage, I guess it could be a welcomed getaway."

We both laughed. "Luckily, we never hit that stage in our marriage where we felt like we needed that kind of break." I squeezed Jim's hand.

"Same here," she said.

She sat up straight. "Although my agency can help with most of your needs, it's important to keep going to the Memory Café. They are a valuable lifeline for both of you. I can't wait for you to attend next week's session. We are going to make a 'memory board.' It's a large cork board you pin your favorite photographs. It's helpful to help hold on to personal memories. We found that seeing the images still evokes an emotional response, which helps you reconnect with forgotten moments."

Watching Jim's eyes light up, I hadn't realized how his dependence on me weighed on him.

"Do you guys want me to help with this?" Vicky asked.

Jim looked at me for guidance. I gave him a warm smile and rubbed his shoulder. "Hon, we've got this, right? This will be a fun project."

He nodded. "Yes, it will be fun setting all this up. Thanks for the offer, Vicky. We'd love to have you back for dinner so you can see our progress."

"I'd love nothing more. I guess that's my cue if you don't need me for anything else. As you implement things, please don't hesitate to call if you have questions or if other issues come up. I'll see you guys next week at the café."

I walked her to the door. She pointed to my yoga mat on the hall bench. "Please make sure you keep your practice up. It'll keep you calm and patient with Jim. Especially on tough days. It wouldn't hurt to add mindfulness and stress reduction techniques like deep breathing exercises and meditation."

"I will. Thanks."

As the door closed behind Vicky, I realized how desperately I'd needed to be heard and have an advocate for me as well as Jim. Keeping my focus on Jim's needs 24/7 was exhausting. Having someone looking after me and understanding what I was going through was like a lifeline. I'd been slowly drowning and hadn't realized it until that moment.

Chapter 10 Jim

Birds chirping in the large oak tree outside the bedroom window filled the air. Nature's symphony gently nudged me awake. I took a deep breath, stretched, rubbed my eyes, and tried to recall yesterday, but the memories seemed far away, like a distant dream.

The morning sun peeked through my curtains, bathing the room in a warm light, softening the edges of the furniture, and throwing shadows on the wall like a puppet show. I stretched my arm across the bed, feeling for Jill. The nutty aroma of the dark roast and the gurgling of the coffee maker told me she was already up, but sometimes she came back in for our morning snuggle.

I loved how the cool sheets felt against my skin as I reached out for her. No snuggle today. I hoped she wasn't angry with me. I couldn't remember what I did. I could only remember her calling me a cantankerous old fart more than once. With a yawn, I peeled myself away from our cozy bed, letting my feet touch the cool hardwood floor. I looked at my slippers. The worn fabric at one time felt comforting against my skin now felt like I was resting on a towel dried in the sun, its stiff fabric poking at my feet. Sliding into them felt like I was exfoliating my soles with sandpaper.

I reached for my glasses beside the bedside table. That's what we did yesterday! I got my new glasses! The now familiar twinge of frustration made its way to the surface. My eyesight had been steadily deteriorating. It was a constant battle to keep myself clear-headed and focused.

Jill and I had fought on the way home. It wasn't because of the glasses. It was an odd uneasy feeling I had being outside the house and took it out on her. I put the glasses on, and the furniture slowly came into focus. The blurred edges sharpened, colors became vibrant, and everything was suddenly clearer. If only there were glasses for my memory.

Even with the fragments of my visit returning, the haze of confusion still hovered. With a determined exhale, I pushed myself off the bed and followed the scent of coffee.

As I entered the kitchen, the familiar sights and sounds of the coffee machine hummed softly, providing a semblance of routine. With each passing day, the simple act of navigating my home became more challenging. I looked around the kitchen and couldn't recall where we kept the mugs. My life had turned into a game show. Each closed door represented a "what's behind cabinet number one" call from the game show host.

Jill caught my confusion, jumped up, and grabbed a mug, quickly filling it. I took it from her and closed my eyes. The heat of the mug grounded my swirling thoughts. Taking a sip, I felt the warmth spread through me.

"Good morning, love. I printed out all the signs with pictures. I thought we could put them up together after breakfast. I've already moved items we won't be tagging above or below your line of vision."

"Oh, I've gone back to 'my love' from cantankerous old fart?"

"Coot. I'm sorry for calling you a cantankerous old coot."

"Coot, fart, whatever."

Jill came over and wrapped her arms around me. "Even when you're acting like an old coot, I wouldn't throw you back. You're my old coot. I've got all the pictures laid out for the memory box. We can put up the signs in the kitchen and then head to the living room to sort out photos before we go to the Memory Café."

"I'd like that."

Chapter 11 Jill

I picked up my book and tucked my foot underneath me. I had a few minutes while Jim showered to knock out a few pages. I'd barely finished the page when he walked in. His shoulders were more hunched than usual, and his movements were noticeably slower. It was startling, but I told myself it was the cooler weather triggering his arthritis. It didn't mean he was getting worse. In my heart, I knew it was wishful thinking. The way he entered a room now was such a juxtaposition from his former confident, full stride that he'd almost become unrecognizable.

"I thought you were going to take a shower?"

He stopped and gave me a blank stare. "I don't need one."

I jumped up, held him by the arm, and navigated us to the worn leather couch. We sat, and I pointed to a wooden memory box with dozens of Irish shamrocks hand-carved across the top, which was resting on the coffee table. "Ready, babe?"

He nodded.

I placed the box on my lap and opened the lid. Jim winced as the hinges made a soft creak. He was so sensitive to sound these days. The woodsy cedar smell of the box almost covered the faint musty scent from worn letters and aged photographs. I removed several albums and placed them to my left. To the right of the albums was a smaller mahogany box we agreed would hold our favorite photos for the memory board.

Jim closed the lid and traced the Irish shamrocks. "That's beautiful. Where'd we get that again?"

"Your grandmother gave it to you when we went to Ireland for their sixtieth wedding anniversary," I said, searching his expression for recognition.

"I'm part Irish, you know."

"I do. Your grandfather was Irish."

"On mom's side!"

"Right." I rifled through the pile of loose photos and pulled out one of his grandparents. They had renewed their vows on that milestone anniversary. The family was gathered in front of a waist-high stone wall. His grandmother was beautiful and beamed the smile of a new bride, ready for life's adventures. I held it out for his inspection.

His smile widened. "I used to love sitting on that brick wall watching the sheep. It drove Mom crazy. She'd always yell at me to get down before I cracked my head like Humpty Dumpty. Mhamó, uh, grandma would always tell her, 'Let the boy be. Bones break, bones heal.'"

I laughed. "That doesn't surprise me. You've always been a bit of a daredevil. Hey, I think I have a picture of sheep by that wall. If we come across it, let's put it on the memory board along with this picture of your grandparents." I lowered the photo in the smaller box.

He nodded. "That's a keeper, one down."

I was so happy he was engaging.

Then he shook his head. I thought he was going to ask me not to save the photo when he let out a small laugh. "I may be part Irish, but I sure have the darndest time understanding the thick accents."

I burst out laughing. "The server tried to be so patient with you, asking her to repeat everything, but then she lost it when you turned to Eric and asked what she said. He told you she asked if you needed another beer, and when you nodded, she screamed, 'I'm speaking English, you cabbage!'"

Jim laughed. "Eric spit beer out of his nose, laughing so hard. He told me she'd just called me an idiot. I lied and told her I forgot my hearing aid and had a hard time following the dialect. She felt so bad. I think I got that drink for free."

"You did!" I giggled as I set the box on the floor. The sag in the middle of the couch from years of movie nights and weekend snuggles almost rolled me into him. I scooted close and opened the first album. We had saved a lot of photos from our days in the school system. This book was filled with memories of pep rallies. "Jim, you were the best thing that ever happened to that high school. When you retired, it took six months to find another principal with even half your skills. Your successor was a good guy, but he wasn't you. The teachers had a hard time adjusting, especially me. It's why I retired early."

"I thought it was so we could travel."

"That, too." I laughed.

He grabbed the photo album from my lap and flipped through a few pages. I picked up a picture of us that fell out. "Is it crazy how much I love this skinny little red-and-white Christmas tree?" It was one of my fondest memories. Jim and I were walking our pup, Cooper, in the neighborhood and ran across a neighbor's yard sale. Jim resisted an artificial tree every time I tried to buy one, but that day, I broke him. It wasn't easy. He loved our annual excursions to chop down the "the best on the lot," as he called our evergreens. I finally convinced him that although I enjoyed watching my "He-man" bag his tree, it made my heart ache to kill something for a few weeks of pleasure. I also admitted to hating the pine needles everywhere. He told me he'd wished I'd shared that when we first got married. It made him happy to see me happy. "Can't we at least get a green one?" he'd asked. I had laughed and told him the uniqueness made my heart sing. After some bantering, he conceded and the little beauty made our living room magical every holiday, with red and white Christmas pillows on the sofa adding the pièce de résistance.

Jim looked closely at the image. "Whose idea was it to get this monstrosity? It couldn't have been mine. I love chopping down a fresh Christmas tree. I remember that."

My heart sank. I raised my hand. "Guilty. We found it in a yard sale when we were walking Cooper. We fought about it, and yes, you loved playing the annual lumber-jack. I told you I hated killing something for a few weeks of enjoyment and that I also wasn't a fan of the needles everywhere. You finally broke down and shelled out twenty bucks."

He ran his fingers through his hair and scratched his head. "Who's Cooper?"

I pointed to our sweet pup sitting between us in the photo. "He was our Golden. You called him the Hipster because he was always at your hip. You guys were inseparable."

Jim's brow furrowed as he turned a few pages. "Who are these people? Are they friends or family?"

I looked at the photo he pointed to. "Family. That's your sister Ella and her husband Tommy."

"I have a sister?"

"Had. I'm sorry she's passed."

His shoulder's dropped. "Were we close? Did I go to her funeral?"

"Yes to both. You gave a beautiful eulogy."

Jim threw the album in the box and placed his head in his hands. "I had a sister, and she's gone. I don't want to do this. I can't remember my own sister! Throwing pictures up on a memory board won't magically bring back a memory that isn't there!"

I rubbed circles across his back. "I know it's hard for you, but we have to try, Jim. Vicky said seeing photos can be comforting, even if you can't remember."

"What's the point, Jill? This box will only remind me of everything I've forgotten."

"I'll share these memories with you."

He sighed, still looking at the photos with a mixture of longing and despair. "I know you're expecting me to remember, but I can't. I don't know who these people are. How's that supposed to be comforting? I can't explain how that feels, but I wouldn't wish it on my worst enemy."

"I don't expect you to remember. I didn't mean to put pressure on you. Vicky thought the pictures might bring some comfort, even if the details were fuzzy or nonexistent. You'd be able to tell from the photos how much you're loved."

Jim nodded. "Right now, it's like pouring salt on an open wound. It's pure torture." He put his hand on my lap. "It's possible I'm having an off day, and I'll really love these."

He leaned back against the couch. "Can we do this some other time and skip the group today? I'm pretty worn out."

I returned the albums to the memory box, closed the lid, and kissed his cheek. "Of course. Why don't I fix us lunch, and we can watch a movie after?"

"Um, maybe we can only pin up the photos I remember? Would that be okay?"

I patted his knee. "That's a great idea. They'll remind both of us of our adventures and the good times we had. I think it's best to do it another day. You're tired."

"I am. Can we try again this weekend?"

"This weekend it is." I ran my fingers through his thick silver hair. "You rest now, and I'll let you know when lunch is ready."

He sighed. "Thanks, Jilly Bean."

I fought back tears, trying to remember the last time he called me that. I knew better than to think he was back. We'd had fleeting moments like this the past few months, and then he'd drift away with a vacant stare. I watched his eyes flutter closed and felt my smile drop with the weight of my disappointment. I had such high hopes for the memory box and our reminiscing today. He was my best friend, and I missed our conversations that lasted for hours as we shifted from one subject to the next. Now, our conversations were fragmented sentences and mumbles I couldn't understand.

I knew there'd be more photos he'd forgotten than ones he'd remember, but I was shocked that he had no memory of his sister. It had been years since she died, but he'd always talked about her and their escapades. With everything going on, I hadn't even noticed she never came up.

I suddenly felt isolated and knew I only had myself to blame. When I saw Jess and Eric's reaction to Jim's odd behavior during game night, my protective instincts had gone into overdrive, and I canceled a few game nights. He might not have full memory, but he still knew how to read faces and body language. He told me later that night he knew they were uncomfortable. By the time I realized how much I needed them, their schedules had filled and we couldn't get back on their calendar. I was getting to know a few members of the support group, but all we seemed to talk about was the disease. I longed for a normal conversation over a nice pot of tea.

Chapter 12 Jill

I walked into the kitchen to take a quick break with a nice cup of tea. I'd just taken care of our clothes spilling out of the laundry basket and the blanket of dust covering the furniture and still had to clean the bathrooms and fold the clothes, but felt light-headed when loading the dryer. My stomach rumbled, and I realized I hadn't eaten breakfast or lunch. I just wanted to sit down and have a cup of tea and a quick bite to eat, but the sight of two days' worth of dirty dishes piled high in the sink brought tears to my eyes. There was so much left to do. I sat at the table and put my head down.

Jim walked in. "Where's my smoothie?" he demanded, a hint of annoyance in his tone. The tension in my shoulders tightened as I sat up. "I haven't made it yet, hon. I'll start now." As I got up, dizziness washed over me again. I held onto the table.

Jim grew more impatient. "You said you wanted me to have a smoothie every day."

Ignoring the pounding in my head, I stood up. "I know, I know. I'm sorry, Jim. I'm making it now." I took a mixed bag of fruit and veggies from the freezer and tossed it in the blender with water. As the ingredients whirled at high speed, I thought about the week we had running Jim to his doctors' appointments, grocery shopping, picking up his meds at the pharmacy, and dealing with the insurance company about a claim they denied. It was never ending. I poured the smoothie with shaky hands, spilling some on the counter.

Jim noticed, "What's wrong with you today? You're making a mess."

My voice had a hard edge to it. "I'm exhausted." I handed him the smoothie and poured the extra in a small glass for me.

He sat down at the table without so much as a thanks.

My cell phone rang, startling me. I picked it up as a picture of Vicky popped up on the screen. I held my breath, instantly remembering I was supposed to meet her for lunch. "Vicky, I'm so sorry, I forgot."

"That's okay. I don't mind waiting. How quick can you get here?" Her words faded as my vision narrowed, chest tightening, making it hard to breathe.

"It was stupid of me to agree to lunch with so much on my plate. I... I can't. I'm sorry, I just can't. I'm right in the middle of things here, so I'll have to call you later."

"Of course. Do you need help with anything?"

"No, I'm good. I promise I'll call you later." I hung up. My hands were trembling. Why did I lie? Yes, I need help with everything and I'm about the furthest thing from good.

I sunk to the floor as uncontrollable sobs racket my body.

"Jill, what's wrong?" Jim knelt beside me and put his arms around me. I let myself breakdown. Looking up through tear-blurred eyes, I confessed, "I can't juggle everything. I should be able to have me time, but I can't. There's too much to do. I'm exhausted, Jim. I can't keep this up." After my tears subsided, I took a shuddering breath, realizing I needed help, support. Vicky's words echoed in my mind, "You can't pour from an empty cup, Jill. Take care of yourself." I wiped my eyes with my shirt-sleeve. "I can't do it alone. It's too much."

Jim kissed the top of my head. "Don't cry. I'll help you."

"That's sweet, but Vicky said she helps give care partners a break. Would you mind if I took her up on her offer to come over once a week for a few hours so I can run errands and maybe even have a lunch date?"

Jim dropped his arms. "I don't need a babysitter."

"I know you don't, but this way you two can talk and she can answer questions."

"I don't have any questions."

I started crying again. "Jim, please. I need this. I need her help."

Jim pulled me in tighter. "Okay, Jilly Bean. Okay."

Chapter 13 Jill

Startled by Jim's frantic screams, I jolted awake, disoriented and confused. Rubbing the sleep out of my eyes, I surveyed the room in search of answers. The early-morning sun peeked through our blinds. I focused in on Jim. He had a mixture of fear and disbelief on his face as he snatched his phone from the nightstand.

In a shaky voice, he answered the ringing phone, urgently stating, "Jim Bish. There's a strange woman in my home. Yes, send the police. Now!"

I hadn't even registered that he said "strange woman." "Did you hear something?" I asked, looking around the room. It was like my brain had a rewind button. *Strange woman?* Then the realization clicked. I watched him, my heart pounding. "Hon, did you hit the panic button? Tell them you made a mistake. It's me, Jill, your wife!"

Jim spoke into the phone, his voice filled with urgency. "Yes. I'll stay on the line." He lowered the phone but still kept a safe distance.

"I don't know you. Get out of here!"

His words cut through me like a jagged knife. Determined to make him understand, I threw the covers back and stood up, hoping my presence would somehow trigger a memory. "Jim, please," I pleaded, my voice trembling. "It's me, Jill. Your wife."

Jim put the phone back to his ear, fear etched on his face. "When will they get here?" Desperation seized his tone.

Feeling hopeless, I picked up my cell phone from the nightstand and dialed Vicky's number. I needed someone who could explain our situation to the security company and calm Jim. "Vicky, please come quick. Jim's in a state and is on with the security company. You need to call them.

You're on the list, and they know our situation," I explained before hanging up.

Desperate for anything to help him remember, I opened the photo app on my phone and held up a picture of us together. "Hon, we're married. Twenty years." Tears streamed down my face.

"I don't know what you're up to. Where's Melinda?" His voice shook with anger.

I held my breath, trying to hold back my tears. "Melinda died a few years before we met. I'm your second wife, Jill."

He sat on the bed and cried for what seemed like an eternity. At last, we heard the alarm engage and the steady beep of Vicky entering the code.

"I'm here!" We entered the kitchen as Vicky placed her purse on the table and walked toward Jim. She gave him a hug. "Good morning, Jim. Are you alright?"

Jim returned the hug. "I don't know why this woman's in my home. She's pretending to be my wife. She has a picture and is trying to trick me to steal from me. I've called for the police."

She stepped back. "I canceled it. She's not here to hurt you. Is there anything familiar about her or the name Jill?"

Jim stared at me and shook his head. "I don't know her. I only know you."

Vicky placed her hand on his shoulder. "Why don't you go get dressed, and then we can talk about this more?"

Jim looked at me. "I don't want a stranger in my house. You'd better get her out of here, or I'm calling the police."

Vicky tried to ease his concerns. "That won't be necessary. Your safety is my priority."

I wiped tears from my eyes with my pajama sleeve as Jim headed to the bedroom. "At least he stopped asking for

Melinda. When he first saw me, he asked where she was. I told him she'd died."

Vicky took my hands. "I won't bring it up. Sometimes those memories are fleeting. He's probably forgotten. The concern is, he still doesn't know who you are. He's so upset; it would make it worse if I agreed you were his wife, and it could make him bring up Melinda again. Should we call an ambulance?"

"Please don't. You know changing environments throws him off."

Vicky nodded. "If he stays agitated, his symptoms could progress. Do you have anywhere you can go?"

I pulled back my hands. "No. It's just Jim and me. I have no one. Vicky, I know you don't normally do this because of your husband and dog, but, if I check into a hotel, can you stay a few weeks? I'm desperate. Would you please? Maybe he'll remember me again. Do you think your husband will understand just this once?"

Vicky gave me a hug and released me. "Don't worry. Like I said, it's not that he doesn't let me, it's our agreement. He'll understand this special circumstance. The longest I can stay is for a few weeks. I've got family in town for Thanksgiving after that. I'll have the agency look for a full-time replacement."

Relief washed over me. "I can't thank you enough."

Chapter 14 Jill

Jim's words echoed in my head, "Get her out of here or I'm calling the cops!" There was no doubt his memory was getting worse; I just didn't think we were at the stage where I was erased. I scrolled through my photos on my phone and stopped at our wedding; the very photo I held up for Jim just a few short hours ago. The one that always brought him back to me. Seeing his blank stare and panic as a stranger held up a photo he didn't recognize was the worst moment of my life. I scrolled through more recent photos. We were laughing at the Memory Café when we completed a small puzzle of a puppy sleeping in a basket. I sighed and put the phone down.

I looked around my hotel room and saw my suitcase and yoga tote still leaning against the door. I didn't have the energy to unpack, and partly, I didn't want to unpack. If I did, what had just happened would be real. I had only been here minutes but already longed for home. My fingers played with my necklace like rosary beads as I prayed I could return home in a few weeks. He'd forgotten me before but always adjusted to our routine after I showed him our wedding photos. We never built the memory board, but from his reaction when I showed him the two of us, I knew even if we had a box full of photos, it would only make things worse. Vicky was right. Insisting we were married would have only sent him deeper into a tailspin.

I rolled out my yoga mat, and within the first few poses, I cried. Yoga not only released physical stress, but it put me in touch with my deepest feelings. In the mix of emotions, a wave of relief and joy at the forced respite washed over me. Vicky could handle Jim's shifting moods, the fights over medications, bathing, and meals as his appetite ranged from ferocious to nonexistent. I could step out of my world of crisis management and tucking and rolling from Jim's mood swings—maybe even meet friends for coffee. My heart leapt at the thought of even picking up photography again. Then the next wave hit me–a huge swell of guilt with an undertow that drowned me in self-recrimination.

It wasn't fair. In a matter of hours, we went to sleep as soul-mates and woke up strangers. Our life together had been erased with the setting sun. I moved into child's pose and let the tears break free. Tears soaked the mat. My mind raced at what would happen next. I laid back in *savasana*, also gruesomely known as corpse pose. How appropriate. My former life, the former me, the former us, was dead to me. I had no friends, no family, no us. I disappeared into Melinda's shadow. Taking deep breaths to settle, I tried to let go of the feelings of guilt and forgave myself for being human.

I prayed Vicky's agency would find the perfect replacement until Jim could remember me. I knew there would be a day when his staying at home wouldn't be an option and was confident we'd find a place that treated him with dignity and compassion. I'd heard wonderful things about several senior living centers in the area. He wasn't ready, I wasn't ready, and more importantly, our bank account wasn't ready. With that thought, I knew despite the welcoming respite, my place was with Jim. I sat upright and dried my tears with my sleeve. Enough of the pity party. I had to keep it together and find a way back to him. I remembered Vicky's advice to never allow the disease to rob us completely, to hold on to the fact that I would always remain his wife— even if he couldn't remember me.

Chapter 15 Jill

I swirled the last bit of merlot in my glass, sending it spinning like it was in a mini centrifuge. Soft jazz played in the background. It wasn't Jim's favorite piece, but it was close enough to visualize him resting on his recliner, eyes closed, enjoying the rhythm. I hoped he'd sense my visualization and was relaxed and calm for Vicky.

The hotel bartender kept glancing my way, his eyes sympathetic. Did he somehow sense the storm swirling in my mind like the wine in my glass? Maybe he learned to read the turmoil of patrons hoping to find answers at the bottom of their glasses.

Maybe one too many burdened his shoulders with their traumas and dramas, turning him into an empath. Maybe he was born one, and this job was a perfect fit.

I avoided eye contact and looked a few inches above him. I could see the back of his balding head and broad shoulders reflected in the large mirror behind him. Rows of colorful liquor bottles added a touch of sparkle, thanks to the overhead light bouncing off the mirror. I looked to my right. At the far end of the bar, a handful of men in suits nursed their drinks, sharing their accomplishments between sips. Or more likely, by the look of their expressions, they were commiserating in their workplace woes.

A young couple sat at one of the bar tables. They held hands and gazed into each other's eyes. I figured they'd head up to their room in short time. Behind them sat two girlfriends giggling, and enjoying the end of the work week.

Traces of happy hour appetizers lingered in the air, making my stomach growl. I had the center of the bar to myself. I returned my attention to my wine, staring into it like I was reading a cup of tea leaves for any hint at what my future held.

The scuff of shoes behind me startled me.

"Jill?"

I turned and saw Eric standing next to me. "Eric?"

He leaned in for a hug. "My God, I can't believe it's you after all this time."

"Eric. It's so good to see you." I motioned to the empty stool. "Please, sit." I held up two fingers to the bartender.

Eric settled in as the bartender placed two fresh merlots in front of us.

"Thank you. Please put these on my tab," I instructed.

The bartender nodded.

Eric raised his glass. "You didn't have to do that."

"I'm more comfortable paying. I don't mean to offend."

"No offense taken." He held up the glass to the light. "Still love a heavy red, I see."

I smiled softly, taking a small sip from my glass. "I do. Bob, the bartender, gives a generous pour. This will have to be my last."

He took a sip, and his smile dropped.

"You don't like it?"

"It's not that. Jess always loved a good merlot, too," Eric continued, turning his wedding band.

The way he emphasized loved sent a chill through me. "Loved?"

"I lost her last year. The big C. A nasty aggressive one. It's been devastating. She was my whole world."

"Oh, Eric. She was so young. Why didn't you call us? You shouldn't have gone through that alone. I could've helped. I could've been there for you both." I reached out to grasp his hand. "I'm so sorry."

He pulled his hand back as if uncomfortable with my attempt to comfort. "We didn't want to bother you guys with all you had going on. My sister keeps insisting I need to move on, and the first step is taking off the ring. I can't seem to take the damn thing off."

I was startled at the insistence in my tone. "Don't let anyone tell you when you're done healing! I know society has some calendar that, at a year, you should brush yourself off and move on. I disagree. Healing's an individual journey. She was a beautiful soul. You guys were so great together. That's not something you can easily get over. Besides, just because she's no longer with you doesn't mean you're not still married. It's not like you got a divorce. You keep that ring on until *you're* ready to take it off. You're on nobody's timeline but your own."

"Thank you. I appreciate that. I was feeling such pressure. It's hard not to think there's something wrong with me for not being able to move on. She was a beautiful soul, and we were more than great together. She completed me. I'm still waiting for time to heal me. I miss her so much it hurts."

"I feel so selfish for thinking all this time our friendship wasn't strong enough for you guys to handle Jim's illness. Here you were, fighting your own battles. I could kick myself."

"Don't feel guilty. It's what she wanted. She would've just worried about adding to your load. Jess didn't want to be a bother and wanted everyone to remember her the way she was. She fought hard and tried every treatment. Her sisters took great care of us."

"I'm glad you weren't alone, and she had her sisters."

"Thank you. Enough about me. Where's Jim? You guys renovating again? I know you usually camp out here when all that banging goes on."

"No. He's back at the house. I'm just having a bit of a respite. It's a long story."

"I've got plenty of time. I'm just picking up an early dinner. It probably won't be ready for another twenty minutes. I just called it in." He paused, furrowing his brow. "You and Jim okay?"

"We're okay; it's not that. I mean, we're not having marital difficulties. I mean, technically, we're not. Mostly because he doesn't remember we're married."

"Oh, geez. I'm so sorry. I didn't realize he'd progressed that far."

"I'm afraid so. Like I said, he doesn't remember me. He woke up and had no idea who I was. He demanded I leave the house or he'd call the cops. That's why I'm here at the hotel."

"You and Jim are soulmates. Don't give up on him."

"I won't. We've had more happy days than bad."

Eric tapped his finger on the bar. "I'd call more good than bad a blessed life."

I nodded.

"Have you been here long? Do you have somewhere permanent lined up? You're welcome to stay with me. The house is too quiet since… I'd enjoy your company."

A heavy sigh escaped as my shoulders slumped. "I'm on my second week. I'm hoping after another week, he'll remember me. Vicky, his nurse, has been showing him my picture. No recognition yet, but I'm praying it'll happen."

"Prayer works. I'll keep you both in my prayers. Is he home alone? I can check on him."

"You're so sweet. Vicky's with him until her agency can find a full-time replacement. I appreciate your prayers. After next week, she needs to go back to her family." I sipped the red wine and let it settle before swallowing. "She's a Godsend."

Eric placed his hand on my shoulder. "My offer stands. You have a place to stay if he doesn't remember you. This too shall pass. You'll think of a way to be there for him. I know you. He loves you so much. I bet he remembers you soon."

"I appreciate that. His neurologist isn't hopeful."

"He doesn't know Jim like we do."

"I'm afraid the Jim we knew is long gone."

The hostess brought over Eric's takeout bag. He checked it and made sure the bag was tight and secure.

I sat up straight and tried to smile. "Enjoy your dinner. I don't want to hold you up. You'd better get going before it gets cold."

"It's Italian. You know that always tastes better the next day. I'm not that hungry. I ordered it more out of boredom than hunger. I don't mind staying; it's nice catching up."

"Actually, this wine is making me sleepy. I think I better head up."

"I understand. Um, since you're here for a few more days, maybe we can have dinner together? I usually order dinner here a few times a week. I'd love it if you'd join me before you check out. Food tastes so much better with friendly conversation."

"I'd like that. I'll set a reservation for seven on Wednesday if that works for you."

He stood and gave me a side hug. "I'm looking forward to it. Get some sleep. You need your rest. I know you're going through a lot."

"I will. You drive safe."

We finished the last swallow of our wines. "I'm going to sign my tab with Bob. You head out."

He stood and grabbed his takeout. "Good night. I'll see you Wednesday."

"See you Wednesday." I watched him leave and waved to Bob. "One more, please, and my tab."

The truth was, I was exhausted and fought telling him I was envious Jess had passed. The finality of death offered a twisted sense of closure I'd never have. She left him with their love and their memories intact. Jim didn't know who I was, and in my heart, I didn't think he would remember. He never forgot who I was for more than a few hours, but with every passing day, the odds were against us.

I know Eric would disagree and say he'd take dementia over death any day. At least then he'd have a warm body next to him. It would be better than losing her forever. He'd be happy to see her every day, even if she didn't remember him. He'd still be able to tell her how much he loved her and could still be able to breathe in her smell. Those are the things I told myself all year.

Bob brought over my wine, and I signed the tab, charging it to my room. I looked at my wine and blamed it for my dark thoughts. It had to be the wine. How on earth could I think it was better to lose Jim forever? Of course, I didn't want him dead. There was still hope he would remember me. I had to hold on to that. Was it my brain's way of coping to think someone else's grass was always greener? I had no business drinking another glass. I pushed my wine away and stood.

This was a rabbit hole I didn't need to fall into. I had no idea whether it was better to lose someone quickly like Jess or slowly like Jim. Both were horrible. And at the end of

the day, deciding which was better was irrelevant since neither of us got to choose.

Chapter 16 Jill

I was surprised when Vicky called and asked me to meet her at the hotel restaurant for dinner. She usually gave her report over the phone so she didn't have to leave Jim. Not that it wouldn't be great to see her and catch up. I was going stir crazy in my room.

I'd eaten half the bread basket by the time Vicky arrived. I looked up to see her weaving through the tables and stood to give her a hug, but she waved me down, leaned in, and gave me a side hug before sitting.

"Did you order already?" she asked.

"Just two teas."

She looked at the bread basket.

I moved it toward her. "The rest is yours. I just couldn't resist their bread and asked for it early. Sorry to start without you," I said, brushing a few crumbs off the white linen tablecloth, stiff with starch.

"Don't be silly. I'd have done the same thing. In fact, I would've probably eaten the entire basket and ordered a second, so you wouldn't know." She laughed.

I smiled, then blurted out the question that had been on my mind since I agreed to meet with her. "Who's with Jim tonight? Did your agency find a full-time live-in?" That had to be why she was here. She would never have left him alone. She was here to celebrate. I was so excited. It was the first moment of happiness I had felt since getting to the hotel.

She reached for my hand. Her eyes looked so sad.

Panic rose within me. "Has something happened to Jim? Is he okay?"

"He's fine. I didn't mean to frighten you. My boss is with him now. I didn't have the heart to tell you over the phone."

I shifted, grabbing what was left of my napkin with a death grip. "I'm glad I'm sitting. That sounds serious."

"I'm afraid it is. Yesterday, Jim threw a plate at me."

"Oh, my… Did it hit you?"

"No, but my agency has strict rules about our safety, and they not only won't replace me, but they're pulling me from the assignment as of tonight. My boss will stay with him until you can make arrangements."

I felt like a trapped rat on a sinking ship. This couldn't be happening. "Maybe he'll remember me now. You know he's forgotten me before, but in the past, after I showed him our photo, he accepted it. It just didn't work this time. Maybe it will again? I can stop by the house tomorrow. I bet he'll remember me."

The server came by to take our order, and Vicky waved her off and turned her attention back to me. Her voice was almost a whisper. She was so despondent. "I was hoping for that as well. Hon, like I said on the phone last week, that night he forgot you, I had to take down all photos of you because he insisted you were an imposter trying to steal from him. Then the next day he forgot what happened. I waited a week and started showing him pictures of you over the years. His memory of you is completely gone."

The floodgate was wide open, and I let the tears fall. "I'll take not remembering that night as a win. He was so frightened."

"I'm afraid it's time for a long-term care facility."

I jerked my hand away as if stung. "I know I'll have to eventually, but not right now. We're just not ready for that. If I pay you directly, can you stay longer? We won't tell the agency."

"I wish I could. My husband and dog are already going bonkers without me, and you know I've got family coming in for Thanksgiving. You really need to consider a facility."

"I don't know what to do. I want more than anything to help him, but he only remembers being married to Melinda. How does he remember her, but not that she died, and doesn't remember me at all? Did he ever love me?"

Vicky's voice softened. "Of course he loves you. I saw the way it beamed from him whenever he looked at you. Sometimes when they remember someone, they think they're at an earlier stage in the relationship. He hasn't mentioned her, so it may have been a blip. The oldest memories hold the longest, but they may not be fully intact or be remembered correctly. His memory loss doesn't mean he didn't—doesn't—love you."

"Then why does he remember you and not me?"

She sighed. "Memories are a tough one. It's hard to know why one memory stays over another. In one of my nursing classes, they described memories like books in a bookcase. The ones on the bottom are the oldest and hard-est to fall off when the shelf is bumped. That's why older memories tend to stick. Dementia, in a sense, bumps the shelf. As books fall, they are returned, but not always in the same order. Eventually, not all make it back on the shelf. That's why he can remember me and not you."

I nodded. It made sense, and I appreciated the analogy. I kept coming back to *he doesn't remember you from that night either*. I bolted up straight, my heart racing with ex-citement. "I have a crazy idea, but I'm going to need your help."

Vicky sensed my excitement and raised her glass. "Crazy makes me nervous, but if it will help you and Jim, I'm in."

Chapter 17 Jill

I propped my worn suitcase against the leg of the kitchen table and tucked behind Vicky, who stood near the counter.

She reached back, squeezed my hand, and let go. "Jim, can you come to the kitchen? I'd like you to meet the new live-in nurse we talked about."

Jim was slow to walk in. The sound of his footsteps stopped at the suitcase. "I told you I don't want or need a live-in nurse. Your company just wants more of my money!" His voice trembled with anger.

I shrunk behind Vicky's back, my heart racing, praying this would work. My stomach threatened to send my breakfast flying. I couldn't remember the last time I'd felt so anxious, and took a deep breath. I wiped my sweaty palms on my nursing scrubs, stepped from behind Vicky, and slowly moved closer to Jim with my hand extended. It was so good to see him. He looked great. Vicky had taken excellent care of him.

My hand seemed frozen in mid-air, waiting for him to return my handshake. As I stood before my husband of twenty years, I could hardly believe what I was about to do. I held my breath, wondering if he would recognize me. My hand felt a mile from his. Decades of loving and caring for this man had led me to this moment. I had no other choice. I moved in closer. "I'm Jill. It's a pleasure to meet you. No worries, sir, your insurance company will foot the entire bill. No cost to you."

My voice was surprisingly calm for as shaky as I felt. For a moment, I thought he recognized me. He was so slow to respond. I was almost convinced he was going to recognize me when he held my hand and looked into my eyes. His warm fingers wrapped around mine and our eyes locked. I swore he was remembering something. But then he released it and looked at Vicky. Before he could say no, I jumped in. "I guess I'd better earn my keep. Have you had lunch? I'm a master of grilled cheese."

He moved to the table and sat, not taking his eyes off me. If he was going to remember me, please God, don't let it be as the stranger who left that horrible night.

Jim flashed his crooked smile. The one that reeled me in decades ago. "Well, I can't say no to that. It's my favorite."

My heart swelled. Vicky's smile was bigger than mine. "I've got the guest room all set up. The first room to the right. If you two don't need me, I'll head out."

I couldn't believe this was going to work. I looked at Jim. "I think with a full stomach, we'll be off to a good start. Jim, do you mind if we try this?"

"I'm okay with testing out that grilled cheese."

Vicky laughed. "That's my cue then."

The corner of Jim's smile dropped a bit. "I don't see her staying long."

Vicky gave Jim a warm smile. "Fair enough. Thanks for your willingness to try."

I gave her the biggest hug and whispered, "Thank you. This is going to work. I know it is."

Vicky tightened the hug and whispered back. "It sure is. God bless you both. Call if you need anything."

As she exited, I wiped a tear with the back of my hand, took another deep breath, and slowly exhaled. "One grilled cheese special coming up."

Remembering the power of music, I opened my phone and played Jim's favorite station. Out of the corner of my eye, I saw him sink back into the chair and relax. I set the phone down and opened the refrigerator. A flood of memories came back: hosting Thanksgiving every year, the table overflowing with family and friends, and, of course, game nights.

I grabbed the ingredients and closed the fridge. As I walked to the island, I looked around. The kitchen, our kitchen, had lost its warmth. The walls normally adorned with photos were bare. Vicky had warned me she had taken them down to prevent him from being agitated after I left. It was jarring to realize I was standing there, not as his wife, but as a perfect stranger.

I focused on making Jim the best grilled cheese ever, buttered the bread on the cutting board, and added two slices of pepper jack cheese and one cheddar. I could feel Jim's eyes watching me. I reached for the cabinet that held my favorite pan, then paused. Jim might become suspicious if I knew my way around his kitchen.

There was no photo on the pan cabinet because I didn't want him cooking. He was happy to make a cold sandwich and didn't seem to notice there was no "cabinet for pans." "My guess is the pans are closest to the stove; am I right, Jim?" I asked as I opened the cabinet. "Bingo." I laughed as my fingers wrapped around the cold handle of the pan.

Jim smiled. "You got it."

As the butter sizzled in the pan and the bread browned, Jim inhaled. "My Melinda made the best grilled cheese. It was the only thing she knew how to cook, but she perfected it. She was my childhood sweetheart."

On some level, I'd hoped the routine of making him lunch would trigger his memory of us. I thought back to the night I had a meltdown at dinner when he refused to eat my lasagna and told me his favorite meal was tomato soup and grilled cheese. No wonder I didn't know. It was something Melinda made for him. I knew they were childhood sweethearts, but now I wondered if he remembered being married to her. He didn't ask where she was again and just shared stories about their prom. I choked back tears. I needed to get past this grief, this feeling of loss, and put my focus on the gratitude of being back at Jim's side. Once again, I could look after him and make sure he was safe. I handed Jim the sandwich. He chewed it carefully, never taking his eyes off me while I cleaned the kitchen. He finished his sandwich, leaned back, closed his eyes, and relaxed to the music. Was he dancing with her in his mind?

Chapter 18 Jill

The soothing sounds and gentle strumming of acoustic gui-
tar nudged me awake. I rolled over and turned off the
alarm, momentarily disoriented, when I realized I was in
the spare bedroom. I clicked on the antique lamp, sat with
my back against the headboard, and rubbed sleep crud from
my eyes.

This wasn't the first night I'd spent in the guest room.
Several nights a week, I'd leave the comfort of my bed and
end up here. Jim was a snorer, and, most nights, I snuck out
after he fell asleep. This pattern increased after his symptoms progressed. He refused to wear his CPAP, saying he
felt like he was wrestling a snake all night. I'd make sure I
woke up early enough to start coffee, cut fresh fruit, and
then slip back in bed for our morning snuggle. I'd laugh as
he'd move his arm across the bed, reaching for me. He hated waking up alone. I wondered if he remembered that
since he had no memory of me. What were his mornings
like now?

My eyes adjusted to the dimly-lit room. The large
cherry wood bookcase, barely visible in the soft glow, was
my favorite. Honestly, I loved everything about this room
down to the Victorian lace curtains. So did my guests. They
called it the Bish B&B. It wasn't just an inviting getaway
for guests; it was my sanctuary for reading, catching up on
emails, playing with photography apps, and knocking out
my morning exercise. I hugged my knees as I glanced
around the room with the eyes of a stranger settling into her
new life as "Nurse Jill". I'd fallen asleep happy that I was
back in Jim's life, but apprehensive that the ruse might
blow up in my face. If he suddenly recognized me, he
might feel betrayed. I wasn't certain we'd recover from the
lost trust.

I placed the photograph of our wedding day in the nightstand drawer next to my wedding ring. I'd fallen asleep staring at it with a mixture of longing for the life we'd built and hope that, on an unconscious level, he'd remember the feeling of our love and trust that his "new nurse" would make his life easier. His words, "I don't see her staying long," were added pressure I needed to tread slowly and carefully not to trigger any anger or reason to send me packing.

I pulled back the covers and made my way to the yoga mat I'd laid out last night before exhausting myself on the exercise bike. After my breakdown in the hotel, I realized I had to heed Vicky's advice for self-care if I were to get through this without spiraling into a depression, curled up in the corner with my thumb in my mouth.

I made a promise to myself that my day would start with yoga and a hot shower before making Jim breakfast and waking him. I finished a series of poses and grabbed my laptop, outlining the day's agenda, and made notes about the week ahead. There were too many variables with Jim's behavior to consider anything concrete, but it helped to at least have a general idea mapped out.

I could hear Vicky's voice. "Don't fret, just tuck and roll with the changes." Thankfully, her agency agreed the plate throwing was a one off and Jim hadn't shown any other outbursts. Vicky scheduled a recurring respite on Wednesdays. Jim wasn't at the stage where he couldn't be left alone because he was a danger to himself or could wander; instead, he had separation anxiety, and any time I left the house, he called me every ten minutes asking where I was and when I'd be home.

She said the behavior was common, and on Wednesdays, she'd come over and join the two of us for breakfast.

Then weather permitting, she and I would settle on the porch to go over any changes in Jim's behavior and adjustments I'd need to make to support us. Then I'd slip away for an afternoon of walking in the park, reading in the library, or maybe even having lunch with a friend.

I thought of Eric. Vicki showed up at the hotel the day after I ran into Eric, so we never had our dinner that Wednesday. Of course, he understood when I canceled and asked me to reschedule when things got under control. I was looking forward to lunch with someone that shared my memories. I knew I also needed to focus on building new friendships. Socialization was a key component in surviving this new life. It was Monday, and like a light at the end of a tunnel, Wednesday seemed so far away, but I knew time would fly and I'd be off to my 'me' day.

I thought about a few members of the support group I'd grown close to. Shirley, in particular, was someone I'd love to have lunch with. We had so much in common beyond our care partner roles. She taught art at a local community college before her husband's dementia declined. Shirley elected to retire early to keep her focus on learning everything she could about the brain, alternative therapies, and advances in treatment. She was fluent in dementia and was bound and determined to fill her toolbox with every opportunity to slow the progression. I loved her energy, hope, and tenacity.

The support group! I made a mental note to have Vicky explain my new role in his life. I knew they wouldn't judge me for doing anything I can to stay a part of his life and take care of him for as long as possible. At least I hoped. My stomach knotted. Would attending the session trigger his memory of us? Should I join a new group? Maybe I needed to wait a few weeks before bringing him?

Another mental note filed away in the "run this by Vicky" section of my brain.

Chapter 19 Jill

Hearing the cuckoo clock chime ten times made me realize how late it was. Usually, the smell of coffee pulled Jim out of his sleep. I'd have to ask Vicky if he'd taken to sleeping in. I hesitated to wake him, but he needed to take his morning meds. Any later and he'd be taking them too close to his afternoon dose.

I turned off the oatmeal, added more cinnamon, and took a bite. It was perfect. Just like Jim liked. I laid out his meds on the kitchen table next to his bowl, moved the furniture around in the den for our morning exercise, and made my way to our bedroom. I gently pushed the door open and peeked inside.

Jim's snores filled the room. Crazy how I used to run to the peace of the guest room. Now all I wanted to do was curl up next to him and take in that sweet sound. It was all I could do not to run my fingers through his thick silver hair and fix the tousles that stood straight like an aged rock-and-roller.

I gently tapped on the door frame, entered, and opened the curtains. Sunlight streamed in. Minute dust particles sent flying from the curtains danced in the sun's rays before floating down to the floor. I made a mental note to toss the curtains in the wash and give the house a good vacuum.

Jim stirred, squinted at the brightness, and raised his hand to block the light. He glanced at me and pulled the covers to his chin. His modesty made me smile. "Good morning, Jim. Did you sleep well?"

He sat up. "You're still here?"

"Yes. Rememb…." Oops, couldn't say the R-word. "Yes. Thanks for giving this arrangement a chance. Vicky will still check on you as your nurse once a week. My role is to help with your ADL."

He ran his hand through his hair. "Help me with what?"

"Sorry to use industry jargon. That's activities of daily living. The insurance term is ADL." I didn't mean to confuse him, but felt tossing him the acronym might give me an air of credibility.

He raised his voice. "I can manage on my own without any help! I'm not incompetent, and I'm not an invalid!"

I held up my hands as an apology. "I didn't mean to imply that. It's just to help with things like your morning exercise, appointment scheduling, and organizing your meds. That type of thing." I quickly shifted the focus to exercise.

I paused and grinned, then said, "Speaking of exercise, are you ready to get moving? Vicky shared your morning routine. How about we get started?"

A look of worry blew across his face. His gaze flicked toward the bathroom. "I, uh…"

"Oh my gosh, of course. You take care of your morning, um, business, and I'll make the bed."

Jim flung back the covers and made his way to the bathroom, closing the door behind him. I straightened out the sheets and pulled the covers up.

Moments later, the bathroom door swung open, and he emerged wearing sweats and a worn T-shirt.

I smiled. "That looks comfy. You ready? We can motivate ourselves by thinking of how good breakfast will taste after a workout."

He nodded. "Stretches first, right?"

"That's right. I've got the den all set up."

"Good spot."

We made our way to the den. I had taken two chairs from the kitchen table and placed them in the center of the den. I sat on one and patted the chair next to me. "Have a seat."

Jim lowered himself into the chair. "You're doing them, too?"

"Yes, my old bones are so stiff in the morning. Do you mind if I join you?"

"I guess not."

"Great. Let's get rolling, then." I completed a few shoulder rolls, and he joined.

"Vicky said stretches help with mobility," I said.

We completed about ten reps and moved to neck stretches. "Let's move our heads side to side and then slowly nod our heads up and down. Let's do this five times if you're up to it." Jim nodded and followed my movements.

"Up for some seated marching?" I asked as I marched my legs while sitting in the chair.

Jim stood and marched in place. "I don't need to sit for these. Just the head movements. They make me a little lightheaded sometimes."

I stood and marched with him. "Excellent. Just hold on to the chair, please. Vicky will have my head if you get hurt on my first day."

He smiled. "She runs a tight ship. She makes me hold on to the chair, too."

I laughed. "This feels great. I can really feel my blood flowing. Keep holding onto the chair, and let's do a few leg swings to loosen up the hip joints."

Jim completed the leg swings and finished with a few exaggerated hip swivels. "All loosey- goosey. The smell of coffee is distracting. I'm ready for breakfast."

"Okay, but can you do the arm circles on the way to the kitchen, and maybe a few wrist rotations while I'm serving?"

"Deal."

We made our way to the kitchen. I was pleasantly surprised to see that Vicky's morning exercise routine seemed to help. Jim's walk was so much stronger and balanced as he completed small arm circles at his sides. I should have had him do the wrist rotations first. The hallway was way too narrow for extended arm circles, plus I'd rather he stand next to a chair for those.

My heart froze when Jim stopped at the kitchen door. His mouth tightened when he saw the pills. He opened his mouth like he was going to pull his usual protest about taking horse pills. I remembered Vicky's hint not to ask him if he was ready for the pills but to engage him instead.

"I set those next to your oatmeal bowl so you can take them after you've got a full stomach." I put my fingers to my chin as if in deep thought. "Let's see, coffee would be too hot for the capsules. What would you prefer, water or juice?"

Jim blinked, surprised by the question. "Uh, juice."

"Lovely, grab a glass for me, will you? I'll get the juice from the refrigerator." I wanted to do a little dance. Just as Vicky described, giving Jim a task and engaging him in the process shifted the tiring fights.

He fetched a glass, brought it to the table, and sat down. He placed a napkin on his lap.

"Thanks." I poured, then paused. "You tell me when."

I filled the glass halfway and stopped when he said, "When."

I had to bite my lip to keep from laughing aloud. At least he hadn't lost his dry sense of humor. I grabbed the pot of oatmeal and spooned a few generous servings into his bowl.

He leaned in and sniffed the bowl. "You added cinnamon. It's my favorite."

"Mine too! Cooking for you is going to be easy!"

Jim took a bite and nodded. He wolfed down his oatmeal and took his pills, one by one, without further prompting. After he swallowed the last pill, he drained his glass.

"Did Vicky share my schedule with you? Do I have any appointments today?"

"She did. No appointments. I thought we'd take a nice walk around the neighborhood. It's such a beautiful morning. Do you feel up to that?"

"Yes. I know you don't know me, but I'm strong. You don't have to ask me if I can handle things."

"That's good to know. I'll be mindful of that in the future. Why don't you grab your jacket and shoes while I soak the dishes and I'll meet you in the hall?"

Chapter 20 Jill

Jim opened the front door and bounced on his shoes. "Let me know if I need to slow down. These old legs still have some spring in them."

I laughed, stepped outside, and took in a deep breath. We made our way down the sidewalk. "The fresh air feels wonderful. No wonder you like getting out for walks."

"I used to take longer walks when I first moved here. It's nice to have someone to walk with. Vicky takes me for quick spins." He scratched his head. "I think I used to walk alone. I probably stopped when I started getting lost."

More than anything, I wanted to hold his hand, like we did during our walks over the years. We always walked our pups after dinner, hand-in-hand, chatting about our days. After the rescue mutts passed, we kept up the routine. "It's a nice area. I like the quiet and all the green space."

"Me, too."

It was as though he read my mind. He took my arm, placed his through the crook of my elbow, and pulled me closer to his side. "I hope you don't mind. Just in case you trip. The neighborhood is good on upkeep, but there are some unleveled parts of the sidewalk."

"Not at all. That's very gentlemanly of you." The ache in my heart lessened. Being close to him again sent waves of emotion through me. The joy at connecting with him dampened the sadness at not being able to talk about our memories of the neighborhood as we crossed through the different sections. There were moments when I forgot I was a stranger walking by his side. I knew this time of day most of the neighbors would be going about their day and it wasn't likely we'd run into anyone. Even if we did, most looked the other way and weren't comfortable around Jim.

Jim pointed with this chin when he wanted me to focus on a particular area. For me, it felt like old times blended with making new memories.

I wondered if he would be too tired for the walk back but didn't dare question his endurance. A wooden park bench tucked against an old oak tree was a few feet up the path. "I could use a break. Do you mind if we sit?"

Jim sat and put his arm on the back of the bench and crossed his legs. "Not at all. I told you to let me know. I used to take longer walks when I first moved here. It's nice to have someone to walk with. Vicky takes me for quick spins. I don't mind resting."

"Thanks." I glanced around, taking in the well-manicured lawns and flower beds bursting with color. "The neighbors seem to take good care of their yards."

"They do. I've been here thirty-ish years now, I think." He pointed to a tan one-story house across the street. "That's Bill and Ann's place. They inherited the home from his parents. Good stock, that family. Bill's a good egg like his dad, and Ann's a generous woman. She volunteers for almost everything that goes on at our recreation center."

I followed his gaze. "They must be wonderful friends to have."

"Not exactly best friends, but we try to look out for each other. The entire neighborhood does."

I felt a moment of panic when I saw a couple walking their dog. I didn't recognize them and took a deep breath. The knot in my stomach made me realize it was a risky move to walk us through the neighborhood. I'd somehow have to spread the word. I thought of Susie across the street. She was queen of the rumor mill. Anything you wanted everyone to know, you'd dropped it in a casual conversation. Add, "please don't share this" and it would spread like wildfire.

I realized Jim was still talking. "I'm sorry. What was that?"

"Bill and Ann know my routines so, if I ever needed help, they'd notice pretty quick if something was off."

"That's very comforting. I'll be sure to introduce myself so they won't be alarmed." The sensation to get back to the house made me want to jump out of my skin. I patted his arm. "Shall we head back?"

"Sure. Did Vicky share my appointments with you? Do we need to go somewhere?"

"She did. No appointments today. I thought we could bake some brownies this afternoon. Would you like that?"

"I'm not much of a baker."

"I'll lead, and you can help."

"That sounds good. Can I lick the spoon?"

"Of course."

We continued our walk to the house, with Jim pointing out other neighbors' homes and sharing quick anecdotes about each one. I noticed he only pointed out the ones that had been living here for a few decades.

Chapter 21 Jill

The heavenly scent of garlic and herbs greeted me as I entered the Italian restaurant. Eric stood from a corner table, eyes sparkling with excitement, and waved me over. He'd already ordered each of us a glass of wine.

Eric gave me a hug that lasted a little longer than it probably should have. I was torn between wanting to settle into the hug I so desperately needed and feeling like it was inappropriate for a married woman. Maybe I was the only one in my marriage to remember our vows, but that didn't invalidate my promise to be faithful.

"Jill! I'm so happy you could reschedule. I ordered your favorite merlot."

I broke from the hug and we sat across from each other. "Thank you. That was very sweet. I'm sorry about canceling."

He shook his head. "Forget about it. I'm just glad you figured out a way to move back home, and it's working."

"So far, I'm home and it's working. Fingers crossed, we don't hit a bump in the road."

Eric handed me the menu. "You said their tiramisu was delicious. I'm almost tempted to order that before dinner."

"It is. My friend Shirley eats dessert first sometimes. She says, you never know when you are going to choke on your meal. Some days, you need to make sure you get your dessert in."

He threw his head back and laughed. "I completely agree! Remember that time at the carnival? When you convinced all of us to try the deep-fried Oreos?"

I laughed. "Oh my gosh, yes! And you and Jim couldn't stop eating them!"

Eric chuckled and slapped his hand on the table. "I felt sick for hours afterwards, but it was worth it. Those things were addictive!"

It felt good to reminisce with someone who shared my memories. Too good. A nagging thought crept into my mind. Is it fair to Jim for me to be here, enjoying myself with our old friend? It was feeling too much like a date. I reminded myself, even though Jim couldn't enjoy or take part in stories of our past, we were making new memories. The guilt eased a little, but not enough. I needed to bring the attention back to Jim. "The four of us had some fond memories."

"We sure did. Those were the days," Eric sighed and raised his glass. "To old friends and treasured memories."

I clanked my glass against his and took a sip of my wine. A feeling of warmth spread through my chest that made me wonder if it was the wine or the company. "I wish Jim still had these memories to look back on."

Eric put his hand on mine. "So do I. I'm sorry you are both going through this. Are you doing okay?"

I pulled my hand back to hold the menu. "I'm taking it one day at a time. I have to admit, sitting here with you, I almost forgot about the challenges I'm going to return to. It's been a nice break from reality, and I cherish our friendship. Talking to you on the phone a few times since I moved back has been a lifeline."

Eric's smile faded. "I sense a but coming on."

I met his eyes. "Eric, it feels amazing to have a conversation with someone who knew me before my life turned upside down."

The server arrived. Eric set the menu aside. "Two tiramisus, please."

I sighed, my fingers tracing the stem of my wine glass. "Don't get me wrong, I'm so grateful I found my way back and I'm able to care for him. But it's not always easy."

Eric reached across the table and squeezed my hand. "I can't even imagine how hard this is for you. How can I help?"

I smiled gratefully. "Thank you, Eric. That means a lot. Although I was really looking forward to tonight, I'm feeling guilty about being out and enjoying dinner."

He released my hand and sat back. "Jill, I know this isn't easy for you. If I learned anything from taking care of Jess, it's that you need to take care of yourself, too. Don't feel guilty."

"I know, Eric, and I'm getting better about self-care. Vicky gives me weekly breaks, that's why I'm able to meet you. But right now, I'm afraid our friendship might become a distraction, and he's my priority."

Eric's expression softened. "I understand. Just know that I'm here if you ever need a friend to talk to."

I smiled and had a hard time making eye contact. He needed a friend to talk to as much as I did, and I knew it wasn't anything more than that. It just didn't feel right. "Thank you. I appreciate that."

The server brought our dessert. "Will you be ordering anything else?"

I looked at Eric to see if I'd ruined his appetite. He smiled. "Do you want the eggplant? I know it's your favorite."

I nodded. "Two eggplant parmesan." I knew it was his favorite as well.

Eric took a sip of his wine and sat his glass down slowly. "I can't lie. I'm disappointed. It's been lonely since Jess died, and reconnecting with you has brought me back to life. But I know you're right. You're a beautiful soul and I could get used to dinners and long conversations, and it wouldn't be fair to distract you from Jim. Promise me you'll take care of yourself and if you need anything, please reach out. We can keep talking on the phone if it helps."

"I will reach out and I'll take you up on an occasional phone call."

"I'm here for you in whatever way you need me."

"Thank you." I was still grateful that I had this momentary escape and shared laughter, but I knew I was making the right decision. We ate our dessert in silence.

Chapter 22 Jill

Thanksgiving was behind us. Jim and I were getting closer every day. The exercises were helping with his balance and strength. We worked on puzzles and played board games to help with mental stimulation and started playing with apps with games specific for cognitive improvement. Music was part of our daily routine and really helped with his agitation. We even danced a few times!

I learned to add purposeful activities to our routine. Jim was my sous chef. He buttered the bread, snapped peas, and washed the veggies for dinner. I enlisted his strong arms to carry and spread bags of mulch on the flowerbeds. He still enjoyed pruning the roses and pulling weeds and always seemed at peace in the garden. We had always enjoyed doing both together. We still had our struggles, but after adopting a healthier diet, cutting out sugar and processed foods, I swore he was having more good days than bad. It took a few months to see results, but there was a definite change. I actually hugged his doctor for recommending we change our diet. He monitored Jim's weight and blood pressure closely, and we all cheered when he took Jim off the first of his three blood pressure meds. In addition to having lower blood pressure, I could say for certain the bad days weren't getting worse.

Our new diet focused on foods that supported the brain. It wasn't a cure. Jim still asked the same questions over and over and repeated observations and stories he'd shared several times. I learned to nod and smile in response, instead of correcting him. He seemed more alert and had way fewer mood swings. The changes we made didn't restore lost memories, but they seemed to slow the progression. It seemed the whole cocktail of what we were doing was helping, and we hit a plateau.

As much as I knew how much our peaceful routine benefited Jim, I still needed to connect with others for adult conversation. Vicky stayed with Jim so I could enjoy my weekly lunch with Shirley. She had been so despondent at our last two outings, and I was at a loss about how to console her. Her husband Carl was doing so well for months and then suddenly declined. He had taken to wandering and staying up all night. I could tell she was exhausted, but she insisted she was fine. I knew it was important for care partners to be there for each other and thought about what made her the happiest. Art was her passion, and today, I had a special surprise for her. I was giddy with excitement and couldn't wait to show her.

I walked into our favorite Italian restaurant and swallowed as my mouth watered like Pavlov's dog at the aroma of garlic bread. Shirley was seated at a table in the corner, perusing a menu. I practically skipped to her.

Her warm smile and twinkling blue eyes always put me at ease. "That's quite a spring in your step. What's got you so chipper?"

I propped a hand on the back of her chair and grinned. "I have a surprise for you! We're not going to eat here."

"What? Why did you ask me to meet you here?" She frowned a little and grabbed her purse from the back of her chair as she stood. "Where are we going to eat?"

"Here. Well, not here at this table. In the back room."

"In the private party room? Are you hosting a party?"

"Nope. Follow me."

We walked to the back of the restaurant and through French doors to a room they used for small private parties. The light scent of paint greeted us. Shirley looked around at a dozen or so blank canvases set up on easels, waiting to come alive with color and shape. In the center of the room was a staging area with a table decorated with a white vase holding sunflowers and a bowl of mixed fruit. To the side of the table on an easel was an artist's rendering of a tree with cherry blossoms in full bloom.

She caught her breath and tears sprung from her eyes. "How did you know?"

A lump formed in my throat. I knew she would love the surprise but hadn't expected this reaction. "It's a paint-and-dine event. They have it here once a month. I signed us up last month when I saw it on the way to the restroom. The last few conversations we had, you seemed so depressed. I know you haven't been able to paint since Carl's been needing more of your time."

I put my hand on her arm. "I can't imagine how it feels after years of teaching art to have it taken away from you. I haven't been in my darkroom at all this year, and it's just a hobby, but it's how I relax." I squeezed her arm. "Vicky's right. We've got to make time for us and not just a quick lunch. Don't get me wrong, I love having lunch with you. But we still need to reach for what keeps us grounded and sane." I clapped. "I'm so glad you like it. I've been busting inside trying to keep it a secret."

"Like it? I love it! You're the best." She wiped away a tear with the back of her hand. "I've been so stressed with Carl. He's really taken a downward spiral. He wakes up at least five times a night. It's either his diaper needs changing, he's hungry, he's had a nightmare, or he's anxious about something. It takes at least an hour to settle him, and by the time I fall back asleep, he's up again."

"Why didn't you tell me? I didn't realize it was that bad. When did he start needing a diaper?"

"Two months ago. I didn't tell you because I know you have Jim doing all the protocols that helped Carl for so long. Jim's progression has slowed much like Carl's did for so long. I didn't want to take away from your experience with the worry that this is Jim's future."

I rubbed her shoulders. "We have to be there for each other; please don't hold back what you're going through. How can I help you if I don't know what's going on? It's true, I'm enjoying the fact that Jim isn't declining and physically he's in good health. We both are. I'm not fooling myself that it will last forever or that anything we've tried is a cure. I'm taking it one day at a time, and I'm focusing on taking the best care of both of us. That includes making sure I reach out to my social connections and support group. Please promise you will share what you are going through and reach out for help. It's critical for your health, and in my opinion, the only way to handle this incredibly stressful path we're all on. Can you get someone to help watch him at night? At least a few times a week?"

"Actually, I'm bringing him to a retirement community this weekend. We're starting with a month of respite care while I get the house ready for sale."

"You're moving? Where're you going?"

"I'm renting a house at a retirement community. It's perfect. They have a full spectrum of choices as we age into their tiered system. I'm starting with independent living. If I haven't sold the house by the time the respite care expires, Carl will transfer to the memory care center and move in with me once the house sells. We will use their skilled nursing and home health care program. They have an onsite wellness clinic, too. They also have rehab and hospice. I transferred a portion of my annuity over to them and will have a monthly rental fee. It sounds like a lot, but we are guaranteed to always live there, even if we outlive our funds. They even have a salt water pool and an art center!

Eventually, and probably by the end of the year, Carl will move to the memory care center permanently, and I'll stay at the house. Because I'll live on site, Carl and I can have meals together in their dining hall. Speaking of meals, they are included if I didn't mention that."

"That does sound perfect. Jim and I can help you pack and get the house ready for sale."

"Thanks. I love you guys and am so blessed to have you both in my life. We'll only be thirty miles from the support group. I won't be bringing Carl, but I still plan on attending. Enough of my drama. Let's get on with this amazing treat." She gave me a hug that made my spine crackle and pop. "Oh, my." She laughed. "I think I just gave you a chiropractic adjustment."

I laughed. "I think you did. Send me an invoice, that felt great. And if you got the crick out of my neck, I'll book a session. "

"A side gig. I like it."

"It would be a great second career. You're a natural."

"Happily retired, I think I'll keep it that way. Come on. Let's get settled."

Most of the participants had already staked out their spots. We headed to the back row and claimed two canvases.

Between each canvas was a small table with two empty wine glasses, and a small charcuterie board filled with meat, cheeses, grapes, and olives. On the opposite side of each canvas was a small table for a water jar to clean the brushes and two paint brushes. We took our seats, and I popped a grape in my mouth as a server came over with a bottle of wine draped in a white linen cloth.

"Madam?"

"Yes, please. For my friend as well." I pointed at Shirley.

He filled both our glasses and bowed before heading to the next row.

The instructor walked over to the table and adjusted a few of the sunflowers. She was in her twenties and had the cutest bob haircut. She wore a painting smock covered in multiple colors of paint splatter and smears. "Hello, everyone. My name is Justine, and I'm so glad you could join us. Let me do a quick count to see if anyone is missing." She stood, pointing over our heads, and moved her lips as she tallied. "Looks like we're all here. Is this anyone's first time painting?"

A few of us raised our hands. I smiled at Shirley as I lowered my hand.

"It's great to try new things. I hope you enjoy it. Don't get frustrated. We're here to have fun, and everyone's painting will be beautiful and filled with memories. Let's get started."

She pointed to a trolley with three levels, each holding several palettes with paint-filled circles. "Raise your hands and let me know which item you would like to paint and my assistant, Freda, will bring you a palette with the appropriate colors."

She motioned to the staging table and easel. "You don't have to paint any of these. You can do freestyle if you want. It doesn't have to be complex or perfect. Van Gogh used three tints of yellow with his sunflowers. It's a simple motif to start with, and it seems to have universal appeal."

She had me at "simple to start with." I picked the sunflowers. Of course, Shirley picked the more complex cherry blossom tree. We munched and painted for about an hour. I watched her smile widen with every brush stroke, and had to admit, I felt amazing as well. I stepped back to admire the vase and first flower I had just completed. It wasn't bad, actually. I started on the stem of the second flower and noticed Shirley had already finished her tree and blossoms. She shaded the trunk with multiple browns, giving it depth. I looked at the drawing on the easel she was copying. She was creating a more dynamic piece than the sample, no contest! I looked back at my canvas and was less enamored after looking at hers. She must have caught my frown.

"That looks great. You're a natural." She beamed as she accidentally dipped her brush in the wine instead of the water.

"Oh, stop, Ms. Picasso. Mine looks more like a child's drawing compared to yours."

"No. It's really good. You're using the perfect yellow and caught the way the petals darkened in the center. That gives it depth, and the lighter shade on the petal's edges creates the image of sunshine on the flower. The green stem is nice and I think your broader stroke gives the stem a soft fluid look. It's nature's beauty."

I laughed. "You're so full of shit, but I love your description. I'll take it."

"Take it with pride, my friend. It's all true. I shit you not." She laughed.

"Man, this feels amazing."

Shirley nodded. "I know. I don't want it to end." She raised her glass and realized she had placed her brush there instead of the water glass. "Look, your painting is so amazing I didn't know my right from left and cleaned my brush with the wine."

I laughed, and took a sip of wine. "I think that was the wine, more than the painting. But let's get you another." I waved to the waiter standing at the corner of the room. "You know, it doesn't have to end."

"I'm sure they're going to kick us out eventually."

"No. I mean, yes. It ends at three. I mean, this fun with paint doesn't have to end. Why can't we do our own paint and dine at the Memory Café? We can ask to have it added as one of the activities. Let's do a potluck and have a 'lunch and paint.' We'll skip the wine since most everyone is on meds."

Her voice took on an excited pitch. "You think Janet will go for it?"

"You're an art teacher. How could they not? You can teach the class."

She pressed the paintbrush's handle against her chin. "Hmm, I have a projector. I can sketch out everyone's favorite photos to fit the canvas to make it easier. Pets, vacation, anything they hold dear."

"You can do that?"

"Yes, it'll be fun."

"Jim has a favorite photo of a brick wall he used to sit on to watch the sheep when he was younger. I'll find the one with sheep and bring it."

Shirley hugged me again. "You're a genius."

"Let me get back to my painting. I've got some catching up to do. You're almost done."

She gave me a side hug. "I'm going to give this to you as a Christmas present if you like it. You just gave me my life back."

"Like it," I mimicked her earlier reaction from what seemed like hours ago. "I love it and would be honored to hang it over my fireplace."

"Don't get carried away. It's not *that* good."

"Look at you being humble. It's amazing. You're amaz-ing."

She waved me off and laughed. "Stop. You're giving me a big head."

Chapter 23 Jill

I put the last ornament on the red and white Christmas tree as Jim stood close by, looking out the window. I fought back tears as I hung all the quirky and sentimental ornaments we had collected over the years. The white lights reflected on the delicate blown glass balls we purchased in New Orleans. We even had little framed ornaments that held pictures of all the pets we had over the years. Cooper was always front and center. Even though all of our little fur angels stole our hearts, there was something special about Mr. Cooper that made his passing the most devastating for both of us. Life wasn't the same without our little hipster by our side.

I tried to shake the melancholy and hummed to the Christmas songs playing from the overhead speakers. I looked around the room, deciding what to tackle next. A sparkly wooden "Believe" sign decorated the fireplace mantel, tucked in by spruce garland with pine cones, red berries, and glitter. The room was taking shape into my favorite winter wonderland. It wasn't perfect yet. I picked up one of our stockings from his sister a decade ago. It was the most personal, unique gift she had given us, but there was no way I could hang stockings decorated with photos of us over the years. Even though the room didn't seem complete, I couldn't risk Jim seeing pictures of us together and asking questions.

Until I could purchase a set of plain stockings for the mantel, I was at a good stopping point and moved next to Jim at the window. "The snow's beautiful. I can't believe we'll celebrate Christmas in a few days. Where did you find such a unique tree?" I couldn't help myself. I knew I was pushing it, but maybe the music and the unique tree would trigger a memory.

Jim turned toward the tree and straightened the star. "I can't remember. It sure is unique, though. Can't for the life of me figure out why I'd buy such a weird tree."

"It's not a weird tree. It's cute." Him not remembering the history behind our artificial tree dashed my hopes. It was probably for the best not to overwhelm him. Things had been going too well. If his memory of the tree and us came flooding back, it could be too jarring. Maybe he'd feel tricked, and I'd lose his trust and all the closeness we'd gained over these past months.

Best to change the subject. I picked up a book from the coffee table. "Jim, I bought a book yesterday I thought you'd like. Okay if I read to you?" I held the book up for his inspection.

He nodded in delight. "That's my favorite author! Yes, please. I'd love for you to read it."

I smiled at his enthusiasm. I sat on the couch, settled in to the red and white Christmas pillows, and patted the cushion next to me. "Okay, then. Come sit."

He rested his head against the back of the sofa. I pulled a festive hand-knitted throw over our legs and opened the first page. "Chapter 1." I read the first chapter, changing my voice for the different characters. Something I knew he loved. My hands and face were animated, adding a bit of life to the story.

Jim suddenly sat up straight and turned his body toward me. I set the book down, curious about what he was going to say. He leaned in and took a deep breath. It was as if he were searching my face for something. I gave a slow exhale and an even slower inhale. Was he remembering something? Had I triggered a memory with my antics while reading?

I returned his gaze. My hands trembled, so I tucked them under the blanket. His words were slow and deliberate at first. "How do you know me so well in such a short time?" Then his voice quickened. "You make my favorite meals, suggest my favorite movies, and now you pluck out my favorite author. It's like you can read my mind sometimes."

I turned my body towards him and considered my response. Could I share my secret? "There's something about you that makes me feel like I've known you my entire life," I said.

I caught my breath as he put his hand on mine, running his weathered thumb over my knuckles. The tender intimacy of his touch threatened to unleash the emotions I'd been suppressing all day. It was so gentle and loving. I placed my hand on his. It felt so good.

He smiled at my response. "Forgive me for being forward. I know it's your job, but I feel you really care. There's something about you that makes me feel safe."

I dabbed at a tear. "Please don't apologize. You're not being forward at all. I miss—love holding hands. This feels nice. I care about you and for you."

"I'm so glad you feel the same way. If I were a younger man, I might fancy letting myself fall in love with you. I never thought I'd feel this way again. I'm an old fart. No happily ever after for me."

"Oh, Jim, don't talk nonsense. You're never too old to fall in love, and it's never too late for happily ever after."

"I'm not exactly a knight in shining armor, and I'm a lot to handle given where my future's headed, but I'd love it if you could stay on permanently. Maybe see where this goes?"

"I'm not going anywhere. I'd love to see where this goes."

Jim pulled his phone from his back pocket, and before I knew it, our song replaced the Christmas music.

"I don't know why, but I can't stop thinking about this song. I'd love to share it with you. May I have this dance?"

I placed my hand in his. "Of course." Tears flowed freely as he drew me in. I leaned in, not bothering to wipe away the tears of joy.

"This feels like a dream, like I've dreamt this before." He pressed his cheek against my hair.

"It's like a dream for me, too, but it's so very real."

He kissed the top of my head, humming to the music.

Chapter 24 Jill

Janet not only agreed to letting us have a munch and paint session, she did her homework and saw the benefits art therapy could have. When she realized it engaged different parts of the brain than language and would be another avenue of expression, she was sold. What surprised her was the possibility that it could decrease anxiety, agitation, and depression and could even trigger memory. Art could unlock parts of the brain, just as music did. She was so excited by the potential, she agreed to add weekly sessions for eight weeks in place of our usual crafts and puzzles. If it was as promising as the studies showed, she would present her findings and request grants for funding future sessions.

Jim and I had attended several group meetings after I'd taken the role of his nurse. Vicky had explained our situation before we arrived, and they all greeted me warmly as Jim introduced me as his nurse. They were so excited to hear I had recently graduated from "Nurse" to his girlfriend. This would be the sixth session we attended since we shared the happy news we were now a couple.

Shirley did an amazing job of creating a makeshift art studio in a back room. It was the perfect spot. The large windows along the wall filled the space with natural light. There was a canvas for each of us already sketched out with everyone's favorite memory or picture. She covered a folding table with a fun, bright plastic cloth with splotches of color. She laid out brushes, pencils, and drawing pads.

A smaller table held a cluster of balls of clay in shades of gray, terracotta, and blue, for those more inclined to tactile artistic expression.

Most members took places next to their canvases, two opted for sculpting with clay, and one member grabbed a few pencils and a drawing pad. Everyone oohed and aahed over Shirley's personalized sketches. We had everything from landscapes to cats and dogs. John, a new member and caregiver for his wife Becky, chose a picture of her in front of a large boulder at the beach. Becky had the same image on her canvas.

Janet switched on the speaker, filling the room with a lively Beatles tune. Everyone's eyes seem to light up, and a few swayed to the music.

Shirley demonstrated a few simple painting techniques. Jim stood in front of his canvas. His smile widened. "Is this the wall in front of Mhamó's house?"

"I think so. I found it in a box of photos and thought it was charming with the sheep grazing. It seemed like a perfect picture to pick for you to paint. You're right. I thought I saw something on the back stating it was your grandma's-uh-Mhamó's."

"That's a great picture! I used to love sitting on that brick wall watching the sheep. It drove Mom nuts. She'd always yell at me to get down before I cracked my head like Humpty Dumpty. Mhamó would always tell her, 'Let the boy be. Bones break, bones heal.'"

"You sound like quite the daredevil. I bet you gave your mom gray hair before her time."

He laughed. "I'm part Irish, you know."

"Really?"

He ran his hand through his hair. "I wasn't always a silver fox." He laughed. "I used to be a carrot top. Imagine that."

"You have gorgeous hair. I bet red hair was just as handsome on you."

I turned around at the sound of William and Sally laughing. I peered over at their canvases. They had painted the same image of a beagle. "Cute dog," I said.

William swirled a paintbrush in his water jar. "That's my Max. Craziest dog ever. We did everything to get that boy trained. The last trainer we tried grabbed his check after an hour and left the house muttering, 'That dog ain't right in the head. I'm out.'"

His wife Sally laughed. "I miss that dog every day. But I have to admit, the house is a lot quieter. He barked at his own shadow or a leaf blowing in the yard. I can't tell you how many slippers that dog went through."

I laughed until I noticed Lisa alone in the corner, drawing on a sketchpad. Her husband Harold passed away a few months back. She still came to the Memory Café to play the piano and sing for us. Socialization was helping her heal, so she didn't need to sit in the corner by herself. I made my way over to her. "Can I see what you're drawing? If it's private, I understand."

She stepped aside from her pad so I could see. It was Harold. "You are so talented. You've captured his eyes, and I can feel that loving smile he broke out into every time you were near. I didn't know you were an artist."

"I took art classes in college, and I sold a few pieces in a handful of galleries, but I wouldn't call myself an artist. But thank you for saying that."

"If you drew or painted something, you're an artist. If you sell something, you're a successful one! There's plenty of room next to us. I know this might be an emotional sketch for you, and that's why you're tucked away in the corner, but I'd love it if you would join us."

"I appreciate that. I think I could use some laughter and company."

"Perfect. Follow me, then. I'll grab your stool. You grab your easel and pad."

Lisa settled in next to me. I turned my attention back to our canvases. Shirley had done a beautiful job sketching the Irish countryside, Jim's favorite brick wall, and the sheep nearby. She left out the more complex cottage.

Jim had started with the sheep, following Shirley's outline. His sweeping strokes of white paint had turned the sheep into fluffy clouds with thin legs. He held the paintbrush lightly between his thumb and fourth finger, moving across the canvas with broad strokes, filling the landscape with smears of earthy tones, softening the rolling hills. The textured wall was now a soft gray block that lacked the definition of the individual bricks. The painting's lack of shape had a peaceful, soft feeling, just like the impressionist masters. I smiled, thinking of him as my own personal Monet. Jim was almost childlike as he hummed and swayed with his paintbrush sweeping color across the canvas.

My brush techniques were more precise. I loved pulling out the weathered texture of the stonewall. I messed up trying to create wisps of wool on the sheep, turning them into cartoon characters. My favorite part was adding subtle shadows underneath the clouds. Neither of us felt pressure to produce the perfect landscape. We were just enjoying the evening. I decided I would turn the corner of the guest room into a painting studio so we could both perfect our new hobby.

Chapter 25 Jill

Jim and I had so much fun at the paint and munch session, we woke up early and hit the art store after our morning exercise. We were eager to buy all the art supplies we needed to build our studio. After working with the sales associate and signing up for a workshop, we loaded the SUV with two easels, several canvases, a ton of acrylic paints, and brushes. Shirley had given us a heads-up that acrylic was the best for beginners as the paints were fast drying and easy to clean. The plus side was creativity. As we improved, we could add various effects to our canvas, either by thinning or thickening the paint. It didn't hurt that acrylic paints were easier on the wallet than oil based. We drove back home singing at the top of our lungs to his favorite songs. I couldn't remember the last time we felt so excited and happy.

I tied the curtains back to let the bright morning light flood the room while Jim unloaded the supplies. He'd already moved out my exercise bike and yoga mat before we left. I did my best to hide my disappointment when I told him to take it to the den. I loved having my own space to work out, plus having it in the bedroom served as a visual reminder to work out before bed and again upon waking. It was a small sacrifice. It was more important to get Jim's art therapy going. Besides, it was no big deal to work out in the den. If we entertained more, it would bother me to have the bike in the den, but those days were behind us.

I leaned our paintings from last night against the wall and climbed the small ladder to hammer in the first nail and repeated the process for the second. I hung each painting and stepped to the center of the room to admire our work. My sunflower painting from the lunch with Shirley was already over the dresser, and now our two versions of Jim's grandmother's property proudly displayed on the far wall was a good start to our budding gallery.

Jim walked in and set the smaller bags down and then returned with the two easels. He stepped into the room and noticed our paintings. "They look great there. I would have hung them."

"I know. It just took a second. I wanted to surprise you. Go ahead and set those in the corner by the window."

He set them down and pushed the bed from the center of the room to the far wall. "There's no need for us to be all bunched up together trying to paint. Plus, we're going to need side… units for each of us to dip our brushes in the water, hold our colors, and snacks."

I looked at my bed in the corner. My heart felt like a lead weight in my chest. This wasn't a guest room with occasional use. It was my bedroom, my sanctuary, my place to read, relax, and play with photography apps. My corner of self-care was getting smaller and smaller.

He noticed my pause. "I hope you don't mind? I should've asked. I promise I'll be a perfect gentleman. We can even hang a blanket between us like in the old black and white movie. What was that called?"

I looked at him, dumbfounded, having no idea what he was rambling on about. "I'm… not sure. Of course I'm okay with this. It was my idea to have the guest room double as our art studio." My voice dropped. "I just thought the canvases would be in the corner, and I'd have a bit more space for me. It's okay, though."

I ran my now sweating palms down the front of my jeans and fought the urge to scream; *I want my room back, no, I want our life back.*

Jim shook his head. "No, not if you're okay with the art studio. I'm having trouble explaining. Sorry."

I locked eyes with him. "Go slow. Take your time."

He rubbed his temples. "I saw you rub your temples last night."

"Yes, I had a headache, but it wasn't bad."

"We were in a large room for a few hours, and you got a headache. This room is small, and it's going to smell like paint all the time. You're going to wake up with a headache every day."

"Oh gosh, I hadn't thought of that." I felt panic rising from my stomach to my chest. My heart raced like I'd just run a mile. "There's nowhere else we can set this up. We don't have a basement, and the den's carpeted. The bedrooms are the only rooms with tile floor." I burst into tears, shocked at how shattered I felt at the idea of dismantling the art studio we hadn't set up. I realized I was putting too much hope that this therapy was going to be the breakthrough to bring him back to me, to help his memories raise to the surface. "You need an art studio! The therapy is an important part of your program. I can sleep with the windows cracked."

Jim put his arm around my shoulder. "Don't be silly. You can't sleep with the windows cracked in the heat of summer or the dead of winter. Maybe two months in the fall. I'm trying to ask if you'd be comfortable sleeping in my room. I hate sleeping alone, and you can't sleep in here, so it will help both of us." He kissed me on the cheek. "I told you I was falling in love with you, but I promise, no funny business."

I smiled through my tears. "You want me to…? Yes. I'm comfortable with that." I gave him a hug. "You're so sweet to think about the odor causing me a headache. I'm in love with you as well. I really appreciate you."

Since Christmas, Jim and I had spent many evenings snuggling on the couch during movie night. I figured we'd eventually organically shift the relationship to sleeping in the same room. It looked like the art studio sped up the timeline. I was more than okay with that. A part of me was afraid he'd wake up and not remember me again, but I had to keep putting one foot in front of the other and stop waiting for the shoe to drop or, in my case, the bomb to drop.

Jim tucked a stray piece of hair behind my ear. "Not as much as I appreciate you and everything you do for me. I had my fingers crossed you'd be okay with this. My next surprise is that I already set up the exercise bike and yoga mat in the bedroom."

I laughed. "And if I'd said no?"

"I would've asked you to pick up some lunch and would've set it up in the den before you got back."

"I'm glad you went with your instincts. I know the bike has rollers to help move it around, but it's still heavy."

Jim did his He-man muscle move. "Not for these guns."

I squeezed his arm. "Thank you, Hercules."

He laughed. "You're welcome. Now that we've got the full room for our …stu… place to paint, let's get it set up."

Getting up early, walking around the store, and possibly the emotion of wondering what my reaction would be took a toll on Jim. The excitement kept his adrenaline pumping, but I could tell he was having a harder time retrieving words today.

Jim set up the easels, and I moved the nightstand between the two of them. "Until we buy our painting tables, we can use this. I'll throw a canvas over it."

Jim rolled a drop cloth over the floor to catch the drips and splatters. He used a smaller piece to cover the nightstand and then placed a canvas on the easels.

He stepped back and scratched his head. "Do you know what your next piece is going to be?"

"Not yet. I do know I'll need Shirley to sketch it out for me."

"Are you going to try one from scratch or have Shirley draw one out?" I continued.

He dropped his eyes and moved his shoulders back and forth. "I'm going to ask her to draw one out."

"Do you know what subject you're going to ask her to draw?"

"I'm not saying I'm a famous artist. It's not why I'm doing it."

"Help me here. Doing what? You haven't told me the subject of your next painting."

"Me's."

"A self-portrait? That's great."

"All of me. I'm going to ask her to start with one of me when all of this first started, before the symptoms showed. I'll do the rest to show how I change through this. If we are going to show the art helping, showing the me's change to document is good, right? Lots of famous artists have done this. I'm not famous, but it's good for our program, right?"

I hugged him. My voice trembled. "I'm so proud of you and your dedication to this." I knew he'd accepted the changes that were happening to him, but wondered at the level of self-reflection it would take to do progressive self-portraits. He was right; great artists had taken this on for decades. I'd heard of a few that had completed progressive portraits as their mental illness progressed. They were powerful pieces.

"Thank you. I hope it works out. I saw someone else do it last night and thought it was a great idea."

"It was Becky. She and her husband John were painting her at the beach. It's an awesome idea. I think this is a good place to stop for today. Let's have a nice lunch and then pick out our photos for Shirley to sketch. How does that sound?"

"It sounds like you've been listening to my stomach rumble."

"I have, but I could barely hear it over the sound of my own rumbles." I took Jim by the hand and led us out of the room. Turning to close the door behind us, I had a mixture of joy and sorrow. I looked forward to the time we would spend together on our projects, and I loved that I would have a beautiful legacy of Jim's paintings after he was gone. My heart was heavy, not knowing how many self portraits he had in his future.

Chapter 26 Jill

I woke up to the sound of Jim frantically searching for something. He was in a panic, moving things off the nightstand, mumbling, "I know I put it here. I always put it here."

"Jim, what's going on? What are you looking for?" I glanced at the clock on my nightstand. "For heaven's sake, it's two in the morning."

"Did you take them?" He leaned over the bed and pointed his finger at me. "You're stealing from me."

I could feel my heart pound against my chest. My mouth was so dry I could barely swallow. *Please, not again.* I couldn't let him kick me out. I wouldn't be able to find my way back. "Did I take what? I don't know what you're looking for. Please tell me and we can look together."

"My glasses are always here on the nightstand, and now they're gone. You took them, didn't you?"

"Why would I take your glasses? I don't need glasses and wouldn't be able to see with them." I leapt out of bed to help him look.

"Well, then, you hid them from me. You're always hiding things from me."

I'd learned enough by now to not react to his accusations, defend myself, or deny his belief. It would only make things worse. "I cleaned up earlier. Maybe I accidentally moved them. Let's look together."

He closed the nightstand drawer, stood, and ran his hand through his hair. "You're always moving things. Stop doing that. I can't find anything."

"I promise I'll be more mindful of moving things. Let's retrace your steps. Every night you put the glasses on the nightstand, right?"

"Every night."

"So, if you put them there and we went straight to sleep, maybe I didn't move them."

"Are you saying I didn't put them there? You're blaming me? I always put them there."

I held my hands up. "I'm not saying that. You're very careful about putting things in the same spot. Maybe they fell." I looked between the nightstand and the bed. No luck. I looked under the bed and found them. I grabbed them, stood, and held them up for his inspection. "Got them! They must've fallen off when you turned off your lamp. Please know I wouldn't steal from you. I'd never hide things from you or steal from you."

Jim put on his glasses and looked around the room. "I hate when I can't find things."

"Why don't we keep them in the case and put them in your nightstand drawer so they don't fall? This way, you'll always have them right where you left them."

"Do we still have the case?"

"Yes. I put them in the kitchen junk drawer."

"My glasses aren't junk."

"I didn't mean junk drawer because it holds junk. It's an expression. It's a drawer I put things in when I don't know where else it goes. Let's move the case to your nightstand."

Jim hurried to the kitchen. I hadn't seen him move that fast in months. More than likely, his adrenaline was surging through him, and that it was doubtful we'd go back to sleep. I followed him and stepped past him as we entered the kitchen and walked to the drawer. I handed him the case. "Here you go."

He took it from my hand and placed it in his robe pocket. "Thank you."

"I don't know about you, but my heart's still racing. How about we have a nice cup of chamomile tea and then try to get some sleep?"

"I don't think I'll be able to sleep."

"How about we chat at the table over tea?" I didn't wait for him to respond. "Have a seat. I'll get the tea. You know what I think would go real good with tea?"

He shook his head.

"The organic ginger snap cookies we bought the other day. Would you like some?"

He nodded and sat down.

"They're in the pantry, middle shelf. Can you grab them while I fix the tea?" He walked over to the pantry, then grabbed the cookies and a small plate from the drying rack. He put a dozen cookies on the plate and brought them to the table. I called out to the virtual assistant, "Play soft music." I inhaled as I filled our mugs from the hot water dispenser.

"That's better. Nice relaxing tunes to settle our nerves." I looked over at the table. "That's a lot of cookies."

"They're small."

"Good point. Half the calories." I laughed. Giving him a task, plus the music, had shifted the energy, and we were both much calmer. I added the tea bags.

"Here you go," I said, placing them on the kitchen table.

Jim put his hands on the mug and held it there. His shoulders settled, and his breathing slowed.

I mirrored his gesture. "I love the warmth against my hands. It just calms me right down. Breathing in the aroma is like a meditation. My mom always said a cup of tea solves the world's problems."

Jim nodded.

"You're not very talkative. Are you okay?"

"I don't want to repeat a story. I know it makes you mad."

I had been so careful to not show my frustration with his repeated stories. I even made sure I had a poker face. Actually, since we started him on a clean eating protocol with supplements, daily exercise, and using healthy oils, he was doing so much better. It took a few months, but he'd slowed down on the repeated stories and questions. His walk was stronger, too. I couldn't say his memory got better, but it didn't get worse.

"I'm so sorry if I made you feel that way. Please don't stop talking. I love hearing about your life."

"Thank you for finding my glasses. I need things to be in the same place."

"You're welcome. I'm glad we found them. Thank you for arranging the cookies. I get things needing to be in the same place, and I was constantly losing my keys until I put a bowl on the table in the entryway. We have a good spot for your glasses now. Don't you think?"

"I do." He looked down and clasped his hands.

"Jim?"

He met my gaze but didn't respond.

"I'd never hurt you or steal from you. I really do care for you. You know that, right? Maybe I moved into your bedroom too quickly. Do you want me to go back to the guest room?"

He shifted in his chair. His eyes grew big. "No. I don't like sleeping alone. I'm sorry."

I put my hand on his. "It's okay. I'll stay. I just want you to feel comfortable, to feel safe."

"You make me feel safe, Jilly Bean. I hope I never forget you. But if I do, I know there's a part of me that knows you're mine. I feel that."

Jilly Bean? Was he remembering me as his wife, referring to me as his nurse, or as his new partner? We had grown close since Christmas and he loved snuggling on the couch. Did that somehow bring up memories of us? We never even talked about me being his nurse anymore. Vicky still came once a week, and he considered her his only nurse.

I swallowed hard. "Jilly Bean, that's a cute nickname."

He laughed. "I just thought of it."

I could barely choke out, "Well, I love it." I needed a distraction before I lost it, so I picked up a ginger-snap and popped the entire cookie into my mouth. "These are delicious. I could eat the entire box." I pushed the plate toward him. "Go ahead and try one."

He picked up the cookie and nibbled on it. He finished it and snatched another, popping the whole thing into his mouth.

I reached for another one and dipped it in my tea before lowering it into my mouth. "Try putting it in the tea first. It melts in your mouth."

He followed my suggestion, chewing slowly before swallowing. "It tastes better that way."

"I think so, too."

We polished off the rest of the cookies. I looked at my watch. "What do you say we head back to bed? I think we can get a few more hours in."

"Okay. Will I be late for any appointments?"

I pointed to the whiteboard on the kitchen wall. "No. It looks like we've got a dental appointment at one. We'll be good as long as we leave here at 12:30. Plenty of time for some more shut-eye."

Jim stood. I looped my arm through his and navigated us back to the bedroom.

Chapter 27 Jill

I was wide awake, listening to Jim's breathing. My adrenaline was still pumping and I couldn't stop thinking about him calling me Jilly Bean. Lots of people called me that over the years, so it wasn't unique. I'd been his care partner for at least a year before he forgot me, so nothing changed about the routine when I moved in as "Nurse Jill."

He was still in there. Maybe that part knew we were married but couldn't bring it to the surface. Maybe Jilly Bean sneaked through. Jim let out a soft snore. I slowly dragged the covers back and eased out of bed.

I needed to get rid of this energy, or I was going to bust inside. To calm my nerves, I decided to read by the fireplace and made my way to the living room. The room was chilly and sent shivers up my spine. Rather than messing with the fireplace, I opened the ottoman to grab a throw and paused when I saw our old photo albums.

I usually did everything for Jim, so I would've been the one to pull out a throw from the ottoman. However, my nerves grew even more frayed that the photos were accessible to him. There would be no risk if I stored them in the attic. I grabbed a box from the kitchen pantry and piled the memories in. I made my way to the hall and pulled down the ladder to the attic. We hadn't been up there in years, and the hinges protested with a loud squeak. I froze and listened for Jim. A gentle snore made its way down the hall. I took a deep breath, propped the box on my hip, and climbed the ladder. After setting the box at the attic's entrance, I reached for the long string and turned on the light.

A small round window at the far wall let in a beam of light from the streetlamp. The two lights created zigzags of shadows. Cardboard boxes were stacked haphazardly on the right. The left contained portable wardrobe containers filled with clothes we should've donated years ago. I sneezed as the dust swirled around me, disturbed after a long time, then settling.

I tiptoed to the back and added the box to a stack of photo albums piled high beside an old bookshelf. I stepped back and scanned the books on the nearby shelves. Some were dog-eared paperbacks, but most were hardbacks. There were hundreds of books. I'd forgotten how much Jim loved to read. How much we both loved to read. I thumbed through them to bring a few back to read to him by the fire. He would love it.

I opened one to scan the inside jacket pocket, and an envelope fell out. I picked it up and turned it over. It was from Melinda to Jim, and the return address was from England. *An old love letter?* What was she doing in England? I shook my head. Jim never mentioned she was from England. I felt guilty for invading his privacy but couldn't help myself. I chewed on my bottom lip while opening the envelope. Inside was a Christmas card with a picture of two squirrels in a snowball fight.

Dear Jim,

Merry Christmas. I hope this card finds you well, and that 1995 was good to you. I just wanted to reach out and let you know that our sweet pup Rex passed away this year. I know how much you loved him and hope you can forgive me for taking him to England after our divorce.

I always enjoyed keeping in touch with you and always thought we made better

*friends than life partners. I think we were
just too young.*

*Unfortunately, my fiancé is not com-
fortable with me keeping in touch with an
ex-husband, especially my childhood
sweetheart. I hope you understand. Your
sister tells me you're dating again. I'm so
happy for you. I hope she's everything I
couldn't be. Wishing you much happiness in
1996 and beyond.*
Melinda

My hands shook as I held the letter. I blinked several
times to stop the words from blurring, but the tears
wouldn't stop. I broke out in a sweat. The room was spinning; my life was spinning. I sat down and put my head between my knees. The numbness in every limb was because
of shock. Anger boiled just under the surface. This piece of
paper had shattered my trust.

I sank to the floor, curled up in a ball, and sobbed. Why
did he lie about her dying before he married me? Was I just
a consolation prize after Melinda? I'd been living in the
shadow of this woman my entire marriage, and it was nothing but a big fat lie. What else had he lied about?

Chapter 28 Jill

The heaviness in my chest and a pounding head didn't help me sort through the confusing bundle of emotions at war with my heart and mind. Last night after reading the Christmas card from Melinda, I went through a range of feelings and at first, I was too confused to feel angry. Late in the night I sat with the inevitable anger before finally crying myself to sleep.

I woke to the morning sun streaming into the attic. I decided to contact a nearby long-term care facility. Maybe not permanently, but I knew they had respite beds to give families a break. I definitely needed a break to sort all this out. Every ounce of energy had drained from me with each fallen tear. It was going to be a long day.

Exhausted, I sat up and rubbed my neck. That and my back were stiff from sleeping on the floor. I rolled over on my knees and hoisted myself upright. I folded the Christmas card and tucked it in my back pocket. It was already nine o'clock, so I made my way downstairs to start breakfast and coffee. I needed a strong cup to gather myself before waking Jim for our morning exercise.

All I wanted to do was grab my laptop to research the address on the envelope and find Melinda. I had to know what happened to their marriage. Maybe she could help me figure out why he lied.

Jim was already awake and sitting in the kitchen. I walked over and started the coffee without saying good morning.

He looked at me with the saddest eyes. "Where did you go? I woke up and couldn't find you."

His vulnerability tugged at my heart. I still loved him, but the betrayal was too deep. I didn't think I could forgive him. Can you still love someone and not forgive them?

"I was straightening up in the attic and fell asleep."

"Why were you in the attic?"

"I found an old box of things and wanted to bring it up. Have you ever lived in England?" His memories of the past were mostly intact, so maybe he could help me figure this out.

His eyebrows knit together as he thought. "No. I don't think so. Why?"

"It's somewhere I've always wanted to visit. Do you know anyone who lives there?"

"No. Do you? Are you going to go to England and leave me?" He moved in his chair and fidgeted with his hands.

I put my hand over his. "I'm talking nonsense. Don't worry, I'm not going anywhere. Do you mind doing your morning exercises without me? I want to get breakfast started. We need to get you ready for the dentist after that. Are you okay to do them on your own or do you want me to play the workout DVD?"

"DVD."

"Let's head to the living room and I'll get you started. That sound okay?"

Jim stood. I grabbed his elbow, navigated him to the living room, and set him up. Then I swung by the bedroom and grabbed my laptop. There was no way I could wait until we were back from the dental office. Not knowing the truth would send me over the deep end.

I filled up my mug and decided I'd heat some instant oatmeal when he was ready for breakfast. I sat down, opened my laptop, took a deep breath, and entered the address using a reverse address program. No Melinda. Not surprising since so much time had gone by.

Since they were married, I entered Melinda Bish in a people finder program. She was deceased as of about eight years ago, but her family members were listed, as well as all past addresses. She'd been alive for almost half our marriage. Had they kept in touch?

Could I reach out to a grieving family and ask questions about her past? Jim's sister had passed, and I know he told her everything. Could she have shared Jim's secret with her husband, Tommy? She was eight years older than Jim. Maybe she was already married when Melinda and Jim married.

Maybe her husband knew about Melinda. I opened my contact list and made the call.

Chapter 29 Jill

Tommy lived a few hours away by train. I wasn't sure what emotional state I'd be in on the way home, but I knew it wouldn't be a good idea to drive. My mind would surely be spinning faster than the train's wheels and not focused on the road. I was certain he could've told me everything I needed to know over the phone, but I wanted to see him, to look him in the eye. The eyes couldn't hide a lie, as my mother was fond of saying. His sister would also have old photos of the two of them since she was the self-appointed family historian. I needed to see their lives together. Would digging into his past somehow heal my heart, or would it shatter the fracture?

I settled into my seat and looked out the window. The rising sun cast gorgeous pink and orange hues across the sky. As a train chugged along the tracks, the landscape changed from a concrete city to rolling landscapes dotted with trees that became thicker and taller the farther I went. My thoughts drifted to all the beautiful sunrises and sunsets Jim and I witnessed over the past twenty years, and all our vacations to charming little towns as we explored new states. Perfect views to match our perfect life, or so I thought. Were there signs I'd ignored? I wracked my brain going over the early years and couldn't think of any. I remembered the first time I saw him in the teachers' lounge.

It was my first week at the school. I laughed, watching all the young teachers hang on his every word. He was so handsome and charismatic and didn't seem to notice them swooning all over him. He taught math, and I educated at-risk kids and special-needs kids. At the time, we were teacher and peer, so when we first started dating we had no issue since we'd gone through all the requirements of notifying human resources. We were already married by the time he became the principal.

Thinking back, he seemed uncomfortable when I asked about Melinda. When I questioned him about how she'd died, he didn't want to discuss her death, saying only that it had been a painful time he didn't want to revisit. I honored his request and neither of us brought her up again. I assumed she had died of a horrible cancer, and the memories were just too awful. It was more likely that he didn't want to build on a lie beyond just being a widower. When you offer too many details, it's easier to get caught in your web of deceit.

I didn't know Tommy that well. Even though Jim and his sister were as close as peas in a pod, and we all got together every holiday, Tommy was always planted in front of the TV watching some game. I wondered how forthcoming he would be, or if he had even been close enough to Jim to know any details. The gentle rocking of the train and lumpy cushion coaxed a long yawn out of me and almost lulled me to sleep.

I opened my thermos of coffee and filled the coffee cup screw-on top. As I raised the thermos, a sharp pain shot through my left shoulder, a reminder of the uncomfortable night spent on the hardwood floor. I winced but continued pouring until steam rose from the cup, the physical discomfort paling in comparison to the anguish of Jim's deception.

The nursing home closest to us, and the one within fifty miles had a minimum of a month's wait for respite care. Because I was going for a smaller affordable room, the list was several months out to move in full-time. I added Jim's name to both waiting lists and put down the deposit. I was making the decision with an exhausted and emotional brain, but the man I thought I knew was as much a stranger to me as the man dementia had turned him into.

Thankfully, Vicky didn't ask questions when I asked her to spend the day and possibly evening with Jim. I must've looked a hot mess because as I was leaving, she walked out with me and whispered "I hope you're doing something to take care of you with this trip." She only knew I was visiting Jim's brother-in-law. I was still processing everything and wasn't ready to share. Vicky was a problem solver, and would dive into the reasons why this was no big deal. But it was a very big deal.

The train was filling up. With every stop, more people were getting on than off. The sound of commuters' conversations, mixed in with the clanking of the train rolling across the track, was hypnotic. I looked at my watch. One more hour to go before Tommy would pick me up at the station. I closed my eyes and shifted down in my seat.

Chapter 30 Jill

Tommy was waiting at the station. I barely recognized him. It had been around five years since I'd seen him and he'd gained at least twenty pounds. He was more talkative than I'd ever heard him. I wasn't sure if he was nervous I was coming on such short notice, or if it just felt good to talk about Ella again. He filled me in on all he had been doing since her passing and apologized profusely for not keeping in touch with the family. He was retired and spent his free time as a director of his HOA. I filled him in on Jim's dementia, and that I was pretending to be his nurse since he could no longer remember the fact that we were married and had kicked me out of the house. He murmured some words of support and knowing about the heartbreak of losing your spouse. I didn't mention that Jim had forgotten Ella as well.

Tommy lived about a half hour from the station. Before I knew it, we were pulling into the driveway and walking into the home. It was like stepping into a time capsule. Jim and I were usually the ones who entertained over the holidays, so it had been at least a decade since I'd been over. Ella had inherited the home when their parents died and she did little to update or remodel. Except for ripping out the God-awful avocado shag carpet, everything else was pretty much the same. The living room was still a mismatched collection of floral armchairs and low-slung sofas, their worn fabric mostly hidden by well-loved throws. Ella and Jim shared a love of reading. Built-in shelving crammed with books filled an entire wall. I knew they had the money for updates. I think she liked vintage and nostalgia and felt like she couldn't change their parents' home.

Tommy must have read my expression. As he rubbed his neck, he admitted, "I know everything's dated. I'm still trying to decide if I want to sell it and move into a condo. Too many memories here. I don't have the heart to change things. Ella loved it like this. It reminded her of her parents, and her happy childhood."

"I get it. I'm not sure I'll stay in our home when…" I sighed and shook my head. "It's just too big for one person to keep up."

Tommy nodded.

I wanted to collect myself before diving into the reason for my visit and excused myself to freshen up. Walking down the long hall to the restroom was like being sucked through a tunnel backward through my life with Jim, then through Jim and Ella's childhood. It was full of wonderful memories, with photos of Jim and Ella, frozen in time at various stages of their upbringing.

I stood in front of Jim's and my wedding photo. It was a shot of the entire family. I choked up at the memory of our fairytale wedding and, until the last two years, our happily ever after. No matter how it started, it was a beautiful life and the happiest I had ever been.

I made my way to the restroom, splashed water on my face, and leaned in to inspect my wrinkles. It seemed like they were now deep crevices instead of the fine lines that were easy to cover with makeup. Now my makeup seemed to accentuate every line and blemish. I'd aged ten years in the last two. I laughed that Jim used to call my wrinkles a trophy for a good life's journey.

Tommy wasn't in the living room when I made my way back. I heard a noise in the kitchen and pushed open the swinging door. He was cutting sandwiches into bite-size pieces.

I walked beside him. "Don't go to any trouble, please. It's bad enough I hardly gave you any notice."

"It's no trouble. Just some cream cheese and cut-up cucumbers. The water's almost hot." As if on cue, the kettle whistled.

I grabbed two plates and mugs from the cabinets. "Sorry, just made myself at home here."

He smiled. "You go right ahead. It feels good seeing someone putter about in the kitchen."

I split up the sandwich pieces onto the plates and filled the mugs with hot water. I opened the pantry for the tea bags. There were several boxes. "Lemon flavor, okay?"

He nodded. "That works for me."

We sat. Tommy said a prayer, and we made the sign of the cross. I was happy he'd made lunch since I'd skipped breakfast, and the coffee from this morning was too strong on my stomach. I took a bite. "Wow, how can something so simple taste so delicious?"

"It's the chives and dill in the cream cheese. It really brings out the freshness of the cucumber."

"Well, this will be my new go-to for a quick bite. I know Jim will love it as well." I swallowed the bite. "Uh, speaking of Jim. I was a bit cryptic on the phone. Were you able to find any photos of him and Melinda? I know it seems odd that I want to see his ex-wife after all these years."

He didn't seem thrown by the ex-wife comment.

Tommy wiped his hand on a napkin. "I did. I have several albums from their high school years, a wedding album, and some scattered photos after that." He pulled a few albums out of a box on the center island and brought them to the table. "You know they weren't married long, right?"

I wiped my hands and opened an album. I flipped through a few pages. Their prom picture caught my breath. There he was, her Jim his arm wrapped around Melinda.

Both smiling and standing close. Their love palpable. I swallowed hard and closed the album. "I don't know much about her. Jim never talked about her or their lives together. I had the impression she had passed, and it was too painful."

"Oh, it was painful for him, but she didn't pass, well, not until a few years ago."

"Did Jim ever ask you not to talk about her with me? Or did Ella?" I picked at the crust of the next sandwich on my plate.

"No. I figured it was poor taste to bring up an ex-wife when you two were dating, then it never crossed my mind to bring her up. Why would I?"

"Do you know why they got divorced?"

He chuckled. "Why does anyone get divorced? They grew apart. They got married right out of high school. That was the problem." He leaned back in his chair. "Just too young, if you ask me. Jim went off to college, and she went to a different college under an ROTC program. They got married before they'd left. I guess it was their way of making sure they came back to each other. They tried to meet on the weekends. Then it was quarterly, then only holidays. They got a place together after graduation, and they dragged it out for about a year. The separation devastated Jim. He tried everything to make it work. Even counseling. He was enjoying his new teaching job here in town, and didn't want to move, but finally agreed to. That's how he ended up where you guys are now."

I continued to pick at the crust until none remained on the bread. Silence filled the air.

He shook his head, then finished the other half of his sandwich. "He did everything to save their marriage. It felt like in no time at all, she said they were just too different, and she wasn't happy. She wanted to travel the world, and he didn't. So, she asked for a divorce. I'll give her credit. She took the blame and said she was the one that changed. It wasn't him. On some level, I guess he felt it was both of them. Because he didn't change along with her, they ended up two different people with different visions of what their lives would be like. She joined the Air Force, and they kept in touch for a good couple of years. When she would come home to visit her family, he'd come back and stay with us while she was in town. They'd get together and have dinner or catch a movie. The whole thing was very amicable. When he started dating you, she stopped coming to our family gatherings if she was in town. It just made sense. That part of his life ended when his life with you began." He sipped the tea. "It's none of my business, but why the sudden curiosity after all these years?"

I felt bad for lying, but didn't want to tarnish Jim's memory with the fact that Jim told me Melinda had died. Tommy always thought so highly of him. "Remember when I said he woke up one night and didn't know who I was and that I'd returned a few weeks later as his nurse? It worked because he didn't remember that horrible night he'd kicked me out."

"I'm so glad you could return to care for him. I know it must be hard not letting him know you're his wife."

"It was at first, but honestly, our routine is the same as when I left. I was pretty much his care partner for the past year before he forgot me. What I didn't mention is that he remembered Melinda. It made me feel like he'd never gotten over her, and I'm doubting he ever loved me." I rolled the crust crumbles into a crude ball.

"Don't be silly. He adores you and was head over heels the moment you started working at the school. He called

Ella and told her his life was about to take off on rails. He told us he'd met the most amazing woman, but she was out of his league. It took a few weeks of Ella boosting him to get him to ask you out. He called her every day and talked her ear off about you and how beautiful and smart you were —are."

I was smiling so hard, it made my cheeks hurt. "He did? He never told me that."

"He was devastated when you shot him down and said it was a bad idea to date someone you worked with."

I laughed. "He was persistent, I'll give him that. He even gave me a highlighted employee manual with stars and hearts around a notice from HR stating it was acceptable to date peers as long as one was not a direct report of the other. I'd ask the other teachers if anyone else had dated him. I thought he might be a player. They said he'd never asked anyone out, never attended happy hours or after-work events. They thought he was a great catch because he was so sweet and supportive of all the staff. I broke down and agreed to have coffee with him."

He beamed. "And aren't you glad you did!"

"Yes, of course. Before I knew it, we signed the HR paperwork confirming we were dating and from there it was a whirlwind romance. We'd been married a few years before he accepted the principal position. Since I worked with at-risk and special-needs kids, another program funded my position, and I didn't report directly to Jim."

"You have a beautiful life. Everyone has to navigate the rough roads. I'll admit the road you are on is tougher than most have to endure, but I know somewhere deep he feels his love for you."

"Thank you. That's very sweet of you to say. And you are right, I think deep inside he felt our love. I left out a critical detail."

"What?"

"He fell in love with me again! We're dating. I mean, not in the traditional sense. We are as close as ever, just not with the 'piece of paper' defining our relationship. It really is like I never moved out. We have a wonderful person who checks on him weekly and gives me a nice break while she's with him. Her name is Vicky. She's at the house now."

I looked at my watch. "Speaking of Vicky, I'd better get back to the train station. I don't want to take advantage of her goodwill. I usually just get a few hours in the afternoon, so this'll already be stretching it."

Tommy reached out and placed his hand on mine. "I'm so happy you have his love again. You guys will be fine. I know I'm not close by, but if you need anything, please reach out."

I stood and gave him a hug. "I will. You do the same."

"Sorry, I'm not much of a family guy. I didn't have the same upbringing Jim and Ella had. In fact, being around a lot of people talking over each other gives me a bit of anxiety. That's why I always distracted myself with sports while everyone caught up."

"I'm sorry, I didn't know. I would have made an effort to make you feel more welcome. The same is true for me. My childhood sucked. I'm glad their divorce was amicable and that they had no kids." I threw that out as a test. Maybe he lied about that, too?

"Oh, yeah, thank heavens, no kids. That's an entirely different scenario. You're tied for life if you have kids."

I nodded. At least he didn't lie about that. "Don't I know it. I'm living proof of how bad it can get. My parents divorced, and they each married someone divorced with kids. We weren't exactly a happy blended family. Mom and Dad used us kids as weapons. My stepdad was a monster, but my mom was desperate not to go through another divorce. She ignored us and called my sister and me liars when we told her he beat us and locked us in the basement until right before she came home from work. He gave us the bare minimum of food and always called us fat."

He took a bite of his sandwich and chewed slowly. My guess was he was processing what I'd just shared. He swallowed hard, took a sip of tea. "I'm so sorry. My stepdad was an abusive piece of crap as well. I'm sorry your stepdad hurt you and your sister."

"It looks like we have more in common than I thought. I appreciate that. Therapy and Jim helped me through some tough times. I acted out as a teen and got into drugs. I got my act together with the help of a teacher. It's why I went into teaching and worked with at-risk kids."

"I'm glad you had someone to turn to. Teachers are angels on this earth, if you ask me. I certainly don't have the patience for it."

"I hit the lotto when I joined Mrs. Fields' class. Her support and a great insurance plan that covered the years of therapy, that got me where I am today." I laughed. "Enough of that depressing talk." I picked up the plates. "Let me clear these, I'll grab my purse, and we can head out."

"You leave those right where they are. I'll take care of them when I get back."

I placed them in the sink. "At least let me rinse them. The cheese will be like cement when you get to them." I had them rinsed before he could protest.

"I don't mean to pry, but you sounded pretty shaky over the phone. Did this help? You seem happier than when I picked you up."

"Actually, yes, immensely. Especially reminding me of my first date with Jim."

"I'm glad to hear it. You call any time or come by whenever you want."

"Thank you. I appreciate you. Please don't be a stranger and keep in touch."

He reached out and shook my hand. "Deal."

Although I was still angry, confused, not quite ready to pull Jim from the waiting list, relief washed over me. It felt good to remember how much he loved me.

For the life of me, I couldn't figure out why he couldn't be honest with me. It was the one thing I felt certain of in our marriage. We trusted each other with even our darkest secrets, or so I thought. He knew my troubled past, my dark side, yet he didn't run. In fact, it made him more determined to make our lives perfect. He hadn't run from my dark side, but the moment I saw a shadow of his; I was ready to bail. The realization was a kick in the gut. Despite the hurt, despite the lies, I knew one thing for certain: I couldn't imagine my life without him.

Chapter 31 Jill

Jim was napping when I made it back home. It was almost 8:30, and I was worried it was too close to his bedtime. I tried to keep him active a few hours before bed. He was prone to staying up all night if I didn't keep him active during the day. Which meant I'd be up all night with him. Vicky saw the concern on my face.

"He was exhausted. I think he'll sleep through the night." She smoothed her top. "Did something happen? He kept insisting that you left him and moved to Europe. I couldn't console him and spent the day trying to divert his attention. Nothing seemed to ease his mind. I almost called you to come home, but I found an activity to keep him busy. After he finished, he fell asleep on the recliner. I finally walked him to bed, half asleep. He didn't even wake up when I put the covers over him."

I burst into sobs. "This morning I asked him if he ever lived in England or if he knew anyone who lived in England. I figured he'd forget I'd asked. I didn't know it would send him reeling. Please forgive me."

Vicky ran over and hugged me. "It's okay. It's my job. I'm used to this. I'm sorry I brought it up."

I reached for a napkin and blew my nose. "It's not that. It's everything. I'm just so exhausted. I'm actually thinking of bringing Jim to a nursing home. More than thinking. As of today, he's on a waiting list. Two, actually, one for a respite for me. Maybe with a break, I'll feel differently. The other list is for a permanent stay."

"You know how I feel about nursing homes. Sometimes it's the best thing, and I'd never talk anyone out of such an important and personal decision if they cry uncle and admit when being a care partner is too much. It's the hardest job I can imagine when it isn't something you walk into willingly or something you train for. It's not something you can walk away from at the end of your shift."

"Thank you for understanding. I knew you'd get it."

"With that being said, I thought things were going great, and he was actually stable. When I was here last week, you said it was like old times. I know he was agitated today, but has he gotten worse since last week? Downward turns can happen quickly. It doesn't mean he won't bounce back."

"No. You're right, he has gotten better or I mean mostly, not worse. The exercises help with his stamina and balance. Playing his favorite music helps with his moods, and he's more talkative. We're benefiting from the healthier diet. We just started painting at the center. He loves it. In fact, everyone in the group loves it. We're even getting a grant to continue painting classes. I've never been happier, since before... that horrible night."

"That's what I thought. So, help me understand what's changed. You were so adamant about not being ready for a nursing home. You don't have to tell me. Sometimes you just know when it's time."

"It's still hard. We still struggle over meals, taking meds, sleeping. I mean, the tricks you taught me help to make it easier, and it's less of a struggle, but it's always something. Nothing to the extent that I would throw in the towel. We're in a good place, but I am exhausted."

"I'm glad you put yourself on the respite list. I wish more people took advantage of the program. It offers a much-needed break. I can ask the agency to find someone for a week. My husband just doesn't let me do overnights anymore." Vicky threw up her hands, realizing what she said. "I don't mean he doesn't 'let' me. It's my choice. It's easier on our marriage." She became more animated while talking with her hands. "I know we can find someone sooner than the nursing home, but that means you'll have to leave if you wanna try respite. At least with the nursing home, he goes there and you stay at the house. You decide. Do you want to wait for the opening at the nursing home? It would be good to see how he does there if you're thinking he'll be there permanently."

"Leaving the house is exactly what I need. Having some time to myself will help me sort things out. When you find someone, I can check back into the hotel. A week sounds perfect. Heck, I'd take a weekend."

"Okay, then. I'll get started on that first thing in the morning."

"Thank you. I guess, in full disclosure, I need to share what triggered all of this." I took the card from Melinda out of my purse and handed it to Vicky.

She looked up after she read it. "Sounds like they remained friends after the divorce. So rare these days."

"It was postmarked from England. That's why I asked him about it."

"Wait, divorce, didn't she die?"

"That's what I thought until I saw the card last night. He lied to me. My entire marriage has been a lie." I started crying again.

Vicky jumped up. "Let me get some tea going."

I turned and watched as Vicky headed to the hot water dispenser. "How sweet you remembered that's my go-to. Actually, my mom's as well. It was one of the few good memories I have of her. She was usually too busy or distracted to connect with me and my sister, but once in a while she'd see one of us was having a bad day and we'd have an impromptu tea party. She actually acted like a mom. She told us chamomile tea was her secret sauce to solve our problems. I guess that sense of calm and anxiety relief was imprinted on me and to this day just holding a cup of tea and breathing in the steam helps ground me. I confess I changed her formula. I switched it up a bit and use two bags. One chamomile and another a rose blend." I laughed while blowing my nose.

Vicky smirked. "A tea cocktail. I love it!" Vicky opened the pantry, rummaged through the assortment of teas, and held up two boxes. "Tada."

"I had to find a healthier way to relax. I noticed it was getting harder to limit myself to a couple of glasses of wine a week when all this started, so I ditched the wine and played with a few blends."

Vicky put two bags in each and brought them to the table. She handed me mine. "Cheers."

I tapped mine against hers. "Cheers."

Vicky took a few sips and put on her serious face. "Walk me through what you learned today. Was your brother-in-law helpful?"

I inhaled the hot steam, and the aroma of rose relaxed me. I blew on the tea and took a full sip. "Yes. I didn't tell him Jim told me Melinda had died. I didn't want to tarnish his image of Jim. He always thought Jim and Ella were perfect. I guess we all did. Turns out Tommy had a crappy childhood like I did. Anyway, he said Melinda and Jim were childhood sweethearts. That's consistent. Jim told me that as well. Tommy said they got married after high school, but went to separate colleges and tried to see each other when they could ... usually holiday breaks. When they got back together after graduation, their marriage didn't last. They were too young, and couldn't handle the differences that developed from living apart all those years. After a year of trying to make it work, Melinda asked for a divorce, joined the Air Force and got stationed in England. As you can see from the card, her fiancé wasn't comfortable with her remaining friends with Jim. I had also entered the picture around that time, so the relationship may have died on its own. That's what Tommy thought. He was never told not to tell me she died or not to talk about Melinda. He just thought it was bad taste to talk about an ex."

"I agree. Very bad taste. Any kids?"

I shook my head. "No kids."

"Can you think of any reason he felt he needed to lie about her being dead? I mean, why mention he was married at all if he was going to lie? Why not say he's never been married?"

"I can't think of any reason why. Maybe he said he was married because he thought it might come up at a reunion or something. Or we'd run into somebody who knew them and would ask about her. I don't know."

"It sounds like it's unforgivable for you? Is that why you're struggling?"

"Of course! I love him, but I've been living in the shadow of what I thought was a dead wife that he loved with all his heart. But they were divorced."

Vicky sat her mug down and leaned in. "Did he make you feel like you were in her shadow? Or did you make you feel like you were in her shadow?"

"I don't understand. How can I make myself feel like I was in her shadow?"

"I mean, did he talk about her all the time? Did he say things like his first wife always did the 'x' thing so great and you can't measure up? I mean, did he compare you? What do you mean by in her shadow?"

"No. Every time I tried to talk to him about her he shut the conversation down, and wouldn't even tell me what she died of claiming it wasn't something he could talk about because it was too painful." I blew on my tea and set it back down harder than intended, sending the hot liquid splashing to the edge. "He just wanted to focus on his future, our future. I never brought her up again. I guess now that you say it that way, I made assumptions because she died and because he loved her so much that she was perfect. Since I was about the furthest thing from perfect a person could be, I compared us. He never did."

"Okay. So that reality you defaulted to, or created is not true. What else is bothering you?"

"Other than the *fact* that he lied?"

"Yes. Can you think of a reason someone wouldn't tell the entire truth? Have you ever done that? Would you want Jim to forgive you if he found out?"

"No. I was always honest with him. He knows everything about me. Things that would make most men run in the other direction. I mean, I had some serious baggage when we met. I thought he was always honest with me. That's part of the reason this revelation is shaking my foundation."

"You never lied to him? In all the years."

"No."

"Aren't you lying to him now? Aren't you pretending to be his nurse?"

I sat up straight like she'd just hit me with a two-punch combo. "That's different. It's so I can take care of him. It's because I love him."

"If he finds out, wouldn't you want him to forgive you?"

"Of course."

"So sometimes there *are* reasons we're not completely honest with each other. Sometimes we think it's the only choice we have and that it's for the greater good of the relationship. Wouldn't you agree?"

I took another sip of tea and coughed. "Well, when put it that way, yeah, I have to agree."

"Hon, you may never know the reason. But what I know is he's crazy in love with you. I didn't know you guys your entire marriage, but when we met, his eyes lit up every time you walked into the room ... every time he heard your voice. He still lights up when he's near you. I'm quite envious of it, actually. My husband says my voice sounds like nails on a chalkboard when I ask him to do things for me!" She laughed.

I thought back to my conversation with Tommy and the fact that I shared my horrific childhood with him and my disdain for divorced couples using their kids as weapons against each other. "I may know why he did it."

Vicky sat up straight. "Let's hear it."

"Every Monday, teachers hung out in the teachers' lounge, talking about their weekend. I'd say over half were divorced and sharing their kids part-time. They would talk about how horrible their ex was—either not engaged or wanting the kids full-time. It was one or the other. I always talked about how horrible my parents' divorce was, and if I ever got married, I'd never marry anyone divorced. I didn't want to bring baggage into my marriage. It would be my first marriage and whoever I chose as a partner's first marriage. Jim heard all that. I wasn't shy about my opinion. Maybe it freaked him out, and he didn't think I'd ever go out with him. Maybe he thought he could tell me after we got together and just never found the right time. But I was talking about people with kids. I mean, they're in your life forever. You can't walk away from an ex when you share kids. Even when they're grown and married, you're sitting together at their wedding. Maybe not in the same row, but you go to all the events for your kids, no matter how old they are. Then you go to the grandchildren's events. It never ends."

Vicky nodded. "I bet that's it."

"Tommy said Jim was smitten the moment he met me. Maybe he panicked with me spewing my anger about being a child of divorce."

Vicky put her hand on mine. "You'll never know, but it's a solid theory. Are you good with not knowing? Do you understand sometimes, a person feels like it's their only option to either not share something or not share in its entirety? I know a lie by omission is still a lie, but sometimes it's what it may take to not lose someone in their mind."

"Did you learn all that in nursing school? I got more out of one session with you than all my years of therapy." I laughed.

She pulled back her hand and smiled. "I think it's your mom's secret sauce that helped us sort this out."

We clinked cups again and in unison. "To the secret sauce."

"Thanks. I don't know what I'd do without you."

"I'm here for you. I may be Jim's nurse but I like to think I'm your friend, not just someone who gives you a weekly break."

"I feel the same. I'm so blessed to have you in our lives and to call you a friend."

Chapter 32 Jill

I slept in the guest room. Not because I was mad at Jim or still struggling with what to do, but because I was exhausted, and didn't want to risk waking him. Then we'd both be up all night. I heard a noise from the kitchen, threw back the covers, and ran down the hall, only to walk in to Jim sitting at the table, calmly eating a piece of bread with butter. His electronic tablet rested next to him. He'd been playing brain stimulation games.

I filled up the coffee pot with water and poured it in the back of the coffee maker. I had already added coffee to the filter before going to bed. Chilled water was the secret to great coffee, so I always waited until morning to add it. "You're up early. Did you sleep well?"

He set his bread down and looked up at me. "Are you mad at me? Did I do something wrong?"

"No. Vicky and I were up late talking and I didn't want to wake you."

"Why was Vicky here? She's usually not here at night, right?"

"You're right." I propped myself against the counter. "We decided to get to know each other a little better and had a girls' night."

He nodded, no longer concerned about me moving across the pond. Maybe he didn't remember being worried about it at all. I certainly wasn't going to bring it up. "Want me to toast that for you?"

He looked down at his bread, then at the counter. "We don't have a toaster."

I pulled it out from the pantry. "It's right here. I was trying to keep the counters from being cluttered." I shook my head at my lie. How could I say I never lied? I kept it in the pantry because I was worried about him burning his fingers or hands, trying to get the toast out. Sometimes the toast would stick and we'd have to pop it up with a knife.

He looked at the board. "Do I have any appointments?"

The star wasn't next to today's schedule. I grabbed the dry eraser and marker and erased the star from yesterday and drew a new one next to today's date. "Sorry, forgot to update that before bed. We've got the Memory Café today. I thought after breakfast, we could do our morning exercises and then head to the session early to walk around the rose garden before we start the activities. It's going to be a gorgeous day. Are you up for it?"

Jim nodded. "That sounds good."

I took two pieces of bread out of the bread box and lowered them into the toaster. "How about I cut up some avocado for the toast?"

Jim pushed his plate toward me. "Sounds delicious. It's my favorite."

I grabbed his bread and tossed it in the trash. "It's a great healthy fat for the brain. Much better than butter."

Jim tipped his hand from his head and laughed. "My brain says thanks."

I laughed. "So does mine."

By the time I finished cutting the avocado, the toast popped up. I grabbed the slices and set several pieces of avocado on the toast. It was already ripe so the pieces softened into a creamy texture. I handed him his plate and put in two more slices for me. Then I put some MCT oil in both our coffees and added creamer. It was not only a healthy fat, but it gave us both a bit more energy to get through the day. We had to start slowly, as it upset both of our stomachs.

I pointed to his tablet. "Speaking of food for the brain, how are you liking the app with the brain games?"

"At first, it made me anxious. I couldn't always understand the instructions, and I just felt anxiety because it
seemed pretty simple. Then I watched the example video,
sometimes more than once, and tried it. My scores were
pretty low. I had to keep trying, and now I get a little trophy
and badges."

"I'm glad you stuck with it. I think it's your competitive
nature that's helping."

"It feels pretty good. There's even a section where I
create my own stories based on the photo I see. The tablet
types the stories as I say them out loud, so I don't have to
worry about spelling or typos. When I go back and read it,
sometimes I didn't say what I was thinking, or it just didn't
come out like I thought. I'd start over and try again. I'm
getting better."

"Wow. That sounds fun. I think I'll start playing with
it."

"You'll like it. There's one where I'm a race car driver
and have to move in and out of lanes to get away from
things flying at me. There's another where I have to memo-
rize the shapes and colors when they turn over. I don't think
I can get good at it, but I keep trying."

"A little better is a win and you're having fun at it.
Even better."

"I am." He pointed to the tablet. "Thanks for getting me
this thing."

"You're welcome. I was happy to do it."

His gratitude and tenacity to stick with the exercises
warmed my heart. It made me so glad I decided not to let
his secret tear us apart. Despite everything, I still loved him
fiercely. Love wasn't always easy, but it should always be
strong. Forgiving Jim didn't mean forgetting or accepting
his lie—it meant I moved forward and chose love over

anger. The Jim I knew had a good reason to hide something so significant. After all, as Vicky pointed out, my ruse of returning as his nurse was built on deception and I'd want him to understand and forgive me.

Chapter 33 Jill

Jim and I arrived early enough to take a walk around the rose garden behind the Memory Café. We saw Janet raking soil in a large plot, bags of dirt piled around her.

She waved us over. "Oh, good, you saw the signs to come out here. I didn't realize Connie had put them up already."

"Actually, we didn't see a sign. We wanted to take a quiet stroll, just the two of us." I pointed to the bags. "Looks like you've got your work cut out for you. Do you need help?"

"As a matter of fact, I do. Everyone's helping today. The weather is getting warmer; it would be a shame to pass this opportunity up. There are a lot of health benefits to gardening for the care partners and their loved ones."

Jim grabbed a rake. "That's great. I still do all the weeding at our home. It's like it never ends. I spend one day pulling weeds and when I wake up, it seems like they're right back out there."

"I know what you mean. My garden is the same and I have weeds coming out of my rock bed that are a nightmare to pull out. It's great exercise, too. I'm glad to hear that's part of your routine."

"Sounds like I should be out there helping him, too." I nudged Jim's arm.

"You absolutely should. It's a great thing to do together and wonderful exercise."

"Jim, can you cut open those bags of dirt and spread them in the plot over there? We're going to start a community garden today and work on it weekly."

"Certainly. I'm strong as an ox."

"Excellent. I appreciate your help."

I raked the dirt around as Jim emptied the bags. We were on the third bag when everyone started showing up. The sun was high in the sky, and I'd already worked up a good sweat. An occasional breeze rustled the leaves and cooled my neck. I looked up at the sound and saw a sun ray coming through a few of the treetops. It lit up the edge of the leaves like a halo. I looked at Jim just as he looked my way. He smiled and winked.

Janet waved everyone over. We stood in a half circle around her. "You're probably all wondering what we are doing out here. I've read up on the benefits of gardening, and with the warmer weather, I thought building a community garden would be a perfect part of our program. Not only will we stimulate our senses, we will work our muscles, get fresh air, and have delicious herbs and vegetables to share. As most of you have seen, the Memory Café has a small kitchen. We can also make fun lunches with the herbs and vegetables. It's a great way to reduce stress. Every week we will set aside a time slot to tend to the garden, then eventually harvest the vegetables and herbs. Plus, it's a great fun social time for all of us. We can call out any insects or critters. Kind of an 'I spy' game for gardening. Only do what you're comfortable doing. If you feel it's too much, just take off your shoes and socks and put your feet on the soil. It's very grounding and good for the body and soul. Get it? Sole, soul."

Everyone laughed.

"All right, after we spread the dirt, we need to make rows and then plant! There's a bunch of plants and herbs behind the bags. Grab a spade and start planting. Jim's done with that half of the plot. Janet nodded to her right. "So you can start making rows in that section while he completes the rest of the plot. If you've got a strong back, please feel free to jump in and help him empty the bags and spread them."

A few of the members went over and inspected the potted plants and herbs.

Janet called out to them. "Go ahead and remove them from the pots and spread the roots a little."

I headed over to the plants. They were in the shade of a large oak tree, exactly where I wanted to be. I brushed the dirt off my hands and picked up a small lavender plant. I breathed in the sweet floral and herbal scent. Lavender was relaxing. We needed to plant some in our garden. I pulled it from the pot and loosened the roots. Next, I picked up the basil pot and brought it to my nose. It was so aromatic and strong compared to the lavender. It had a peppery, clove smell. I couldn't wait to try it on a fresh tomato.

I glanced at Jim to make sure he wasn't overheating. He leaned on a rake and laughed at something one of the husbands had said. Janet was a genius. Everyone was relaxed and talking to each other.

Jim pointed to a blue jay on a branch. "I spy a blue jay."

William hollered, "I spy his dinner! A juicy earthworm." He laughed and held up the wiggly creature, then set it down.

"I bet he wants that worm," Janet said.

"I bet he does. It's a fat one," William said.

After an hour, we took a break on folding chairs and enjoyed some lemonade in the shade. There was no set agenda or topic of discussion. We talked and laughed.

Janet picked up a rosemary plant. "Pass that around and take a good inhale."

I was sitting next to her and was the first to receive the plant. "It's kinda woody and invigorating. I can't wait to put it on a piece of focaccia bread." I pinched a piece off and handed the pot to Jim.

"It's a nice, bold smell. I'm down with the focaccia bread." He passed it to William.

"Powerful but nice." William gave it to Sally.

Janet shared the benefits of rosemary as we passed the plant around. "It's not just for cooking. It's also used for aromatherapy and is said to improve cognitive function, reduce stress and anxiety, and can even boost the immune system. That's why I have so many of these. We are going to plant them in whiskey barrels. They are hardy and will get fairly large."

We finished our break and spent the next hour spacing and planting the starters. Shirley, Jim and I laughed about creating a container garden on our deck with dozens of rosemary bushes.

Jim laughed. "I'll sit out there all day and stick pieces in my nose if it'll help."

Shirley shoved a piece near her nose. "By George, I do believe it's working already. That smell went straight to my brain and opened my sinuses wide open."

We laughed.

Chapter 34 Jim

I pulled my shirt on and tried to align the buttons with the holes before I started buttoning it. My fingers felt heavy and thick. It took forever. By the time I'd finished, my shoulders were tight. My muscles were so weak they hurt just getting dressed. I wanted to throw something in frustration. Then I remembered gardening. My muscles were still sore; that was all. A good sore, like when I used to lift weights. I rubbed at my neck.

It felt great to work in the garden and see everyone's hard work at the end. I'd been a jumble of nerves lately. Something was up with Jill, but she wouldn't talk to me. It was hard for me to communicate and remember what I'd already said or even what she'd said. There were still days where I felt like I couldn't be any clearer and was so confused when she didn't understand what I was trying to say. It made me nervous to say anything at all which froze my brain. Then it proved even harder to get the words out. I was so relaxed doing the gardening; it was easier to talk to everyone. Working together kept things on track.

I loved pulling weeds and working in my garden, but most of the time I'd get distracted when going to the shed for a tool. I'd end up puttering around in there and start a new task. Then when I walked out and saw the weeds, I'd remember pulling them. I usually couldn't remember why I went to the shed and would pull weeds again. Then, I'd recall what I wanted, end up in the shed again and it started all over. I was putting things away or just scratching my head about being there. Thus it took most of the day to pull weeds.

I needed to talk to Jill about it. She'd be able to figure out a way to keep me on track. She was always researching anything that could keep me from getting worse. At first, it frustrated me that I kept having to try new things. I didn't like change, or learning new things. I wasn't sure if I was always that way and it just got worse, or if this was a whole new me that my old self wouldn't recognize. Sometimes I knew who I was inside and was the same me, but couldn't express it. Would there be a point when I'd have a zombie brain and not have any thoughts about what I'd lost or felt about this strange new person I'd become? Would I even know the difference, that there was an old me long gone? I still felt strong and capable most days, but other days, beaten down and exhausted.

The first time I tried the brain games on the tablet, I couldn't even figure out what the instructions were asking me to do. I'd watch the examples over and over, then try. I'd want to throw the tablet when I couldn't remember if I was to focus on the color or the shape as it moved across the screen. There were some games I had to skip. It was too stressful and a reminder of how much I'd lost. There had to be a time when I could have breezed through all the exercises. But when I saw improvements, I got hooked. I grew up playing sports and being competitive, even with my grades. I loved the race car game. Sometimes I didn't know why I loved it so much and sometimes, I knew it was because of my love for driving and the freedom and control behind the wheel.

I looked out the window and saw Jill outside in the garden, wiping sweat from her brow. She had pots and bags of dirt around her. I put on my slip-on shoes, headed out to join her, opened the patio door, and waved. She looked up from the pot she was filling. "Did you have a good nap?"

"Yes. The exercises this morning wiped me out. I'm not sure why I got so tired."

"We had a full day yesterday. I was tempted to join you but wanted to get started on our garden. I just have a few more pots to fill. I picked up a bunch of rosemary plants at the garden center this morning. They smell great."

She tore off a piece for me and handed it to me. I sniffed it. "That's strong. Need some help?"

"Sure, if you're not too sore from yesterday."

"I'm sore, but not bad."

"You're in better shape than I am. I could hardly move when I first got out of bed."

"You okay?"

"It's better now since the stretches this morning, plus I've been up and moving around. Do you wanna plant the rosemary in the pots I've already filled or add dirt to the pots I haven't got to yet?"

"I'll grab the dirt and fill the pots."

"Thank you, my Hercules."

I flexed my muscles. "These bad boys still have some life in them."

She laughed. "Yeah, they do."

I grabbed a bag of dirt and tore it open. "How much dirt goes in?"

"Fill it to about the length of your hand from the top of the pot."

I filled the pot. "What's next? Do you want me to add the plant?"

"Can you fill the other two pots first?"

"Yeah, that's right. Fill the pots." I finished the second pot and set the bag down. "Jill, do you have any ideas that would keep me from going to the shed?"

"Why do you want to go to the shed? I have everything you need here. I have the dirt, shovel, and spade. Is there something I missed?"

"I don't think so. It's just when I pull weeds, I keep feeling like I have to go to the shed and then can't remember why I'm in the shed. Then I start straightening up or just stand there, trying to remember what I came for."

"I do that, too. So I got this little apron to hold my gloves, spades, and hand rake. When I feel like I need one of the tools, I grab it from the pocket. When I'm done, it goes in the little roller seat you got me."

"I got you a rolling seat? When did I do that?"

Jill dropped the plant she was holding. "Uh, I meant I got me. Why don't you use my apron when you pull weeds? I think that'll keep you from going to the shed. It has everything you need, even a pointy weed puller."

"Guys don't wear aprons."

"Guys who garden do. Think of it as a specialized tool belt."

"I *could* wear a specialized garden tool belt."

Jill removed her tool belt and wrapped it around me. "Perfect. You look like a master gardener."

The weight felt good. "My mom was a master gardener. I used to help her all the time."

"She was? What kind of things did she have in her garden?"

"She had everything. Along each fence line she had a raised bed with trees. She had orange trees, lemon trees, avocado trees. In between the trees, she had bushes and plants. You'd have loved her sunflowers. They were beautiful. She grew the best cucumbers. Her tomatoes were prize-winning. She's how I got my green thumb."

"Did you plant these ornamental trees? Their beautiful spring blossoms are just starting to pop."

"I can't remember," I said, pointing to the row of trees. "Those are dogwoods and that one is a Japanese maple.

Maybe I put those cobblestone pavers down next to the wooden chairs and table?"

"You've built a peaceful haven. I love coming out here and listening to the birds. Why don't we do what your mom did and scatter plants and vegetables around the trees? I love cucumbers and tomatoes. How about I pick us up some plants and we add those to our garden? I was thinking we'd make a beautiful container garden with colorful pots to surround the deck. But maybe we could build a raised bed along the trees and add a raised bed each year."

"That would be great. I like the pots, too. Can we do both?"

"Of course. Do you want to go to the garden center with me?"

"Yes. That would be fun."

"Excellent. Then maybe we can stop for lunch on the way home."

Chapter 35 Jill

I cracked the bedroom door to look in on Jim. He was still sound asleep. I wanted to wake him from his nap so he wouldn't be up all night. His chest rose and fell and I listened to his gentle snoring. The trip to the garden shop this morning had completely worn him out. He enjoyed himself, but midway through our shopping, he was slowing and, at one point, he asked me why we were there. I was so caught up in the joy of our new garden that I forgot changes in our routine threw him off. We picked up lunch to eat at the house. Both the center and restaurant would be overkill. The fresh air and physical labor helped build his appetite. He finished his entire lunch, and I tucked him in with a promise I wouldn't work in the garden without him.

I pulled the covers over his broad chest. To look at him, you'd never know he wasn't aging gracefully like most of us. He was as lean and strong as ever; he just tired easier after exertion, and his movements slowed. I learned from the group that dementia affects everyone differently and how a person progresses can vary widely. Mostly, Jim hadn't progressed to the middle stage where his motor ability declined. You could say he'd dipped his toe in it, as his shuffle became prominent when he grew exhausted. But most days, it wouldn't be noticeable to anyone that didn't know him as a younger man.

At six foot two inches, Jim had always been an imposing figure, his broad shoulders and muscular frame a testament to his daily weight training. Even now, with his hair more silver than the deep red of his youth, he still exuded an air of strength and vitality. We walked several miles a day prior to the diagnosis and on good days, we could still knock out a mile or two. We adjusted his workouts as he progressed and added more gentle tai-chi-movements, but rarely missed a day. One of my favorite parts of the support group is their motto, "movement and food are medicine." Jim and the other members began their weekly sessions with light exercises when the care partners broke off for their sessions. According to the research, his active lifestyle and clean eating could be what helped slow his decline. I was grateful he still loved being active and didn't fight me on our daily exercises, as some care partners in the group experienced.

Coming out of my thoughts, I closed the door and made my way to our art studio.

When I opened the door, my eyes landed on Jim's paint-spattered stool and then his canvas. A lump caught in my throat. He was further along than I thought. He must have worked on it during Vicky's visit. Every time I walked in, a mixture of joy and sorrow filled me. Today was no different. Jim had always been a gifted sketch artist. Although it had been a decade since he'd sketched, he transitioned to painting as though doing it for years. I breathed in the co-mingled paint odor and the faint smell of cinnamon potpourri left over from the holiday decorations.

Becky's self-portrait at the Memory Café must have inspired him. The canvas in front of me held the first in the series to capture his descent into dementia. I stood entranced in front of the canvas and traced the edges of his brushstrokes. The texture was rough against my fingertips. I rested my fingers on his lips. His smile was as faint as the shades of red and orange he had used to capture the color of his lips. His work didn't have the strong, defined lines that his prior sketches held. It was less like Vermeer and more in the style of a Monet.

These new strokes were a swirling blur of colors, slightly distorted, but organized enough to clearly see it was my dear husband. I couldn't stop staring at his eyes. The vibrant hazel hue I still saw so clearly in my mind when I thought of him now dimmed with a blend of white. His eyes were how I gauged his pain, alertness, and awareness. It was as if he too recognized his eyes were a mirror of the dimming essence of who he was, as more than just his fading memory. The question I asked myself every time seeing his portrait surfaced. I blinked at the tears forming. How many more annual self-portraits would he have?

I looked at my canvas propped on an easel next to the window. I'd never gain the skills to paint from scratch and would more than likely always rely on Shirley's sketches, kind of like an advanced paint-by-numbers method. My canvas was a third filled in with paint. She'd sketched our beloved Cooper sleeping in his multi-colored doggie bed with his arm cradling his pink toy monkey like a cherished friend. Jim didn't recognize him when we were organizing photos the night before he forgot me, so I thought it was a safe choice. I smiled at that silly monkey. We'd bought it for him when he was a pup. It had faux fur to mimic a littermate. I brought it to the breeder when we first picked out Cooper. She kept it in their play pen so he would have familiar smells when he came to our home. I also gave them a T-shirt Jim and I took turns sleeping in, so we'd smell familiar when he joined our family. Both the T-shirt and toy were handed back to us when he was old enough to join our family. The plan worked, and he not only adjusted quickly to his new surroundings, that monkey was the only toy he never destroyed as he got older.

I reached for my palette and completed the first layer of vibrant red for his bed. I bought it on a whim one year to match our skinny little red and white Christmas tree and decided to use it year round. Our home decorations had very little red. The color was harsh and too invigorating. Our daily lives outside of our home were full throttle, and I wanted our home to be a calm, soothing haven and always selected soft, neutral colors. When we set up the bed for him, I realized there was something about a splash of red that brought subtle energy to the room.

Before I knew it, an hour passed. With each stroke, sweet Cooper emerged. I laughed. The sweet sleeping pup resting on my canvas bore no resemblance to the high-strung puppy that would emerge from that deep slumber. The pup I remembered was like a commando, brutalizing my shoes and anything left within his reach for the first few years of his life. I had to be the one to finish the painting in its entirety to claim it as my own, but the urge to have Shirley fill in his golden fur so I wouldn't ruin it was so strong, I left it for last. I used a blend of black and white to complete his nose and added a bit of yellow to the blend when getting to his eyes. Just like Jim's painting, I froze at the eyes. I didn't have the skill to capture his soulful eyes, but they were definitely his.

I remembered the shock of learning Cooper's body was riddled with cancer. He had given no indication he was that sick. One morning, he had skipped breakfast, and for him, that alone was cause for a trip to the vet. Of all our pups, Cooper was the most obsessed with food and treats. A diagnostic test revealed a small lump in his stomach area. The vet explained it was common in dogs his age and could be removed with surgery, with the assurance he'd be back on his feet in no time. We received a call from the vet a few hours after we dropped him off; they explained when they opened him, his body was full of cancer, and recommended putting him down. We were devastated. A few years later, when I was organizing photos in an album, I noticed the change in Cooper's eyes. The last few years, the sparkle and energy that used to radiate from his eyes had grown dimmer and dimmer. I could have kicked myself for not noticing. I now monitored Jim's eyes closely, looking not only through the window of his soul, but trying to see what they revealed about where he was in the process of dementia.

After completing Cooper's velvety ears and the white tip on his tail, our sweet fur baby came to life in front of me. My confidence grew. I blended the colors that would best show off his beautiful golden fur. The door opened, and Jim popped his head in.

"There you are." He walked over to me and put his hand on my shoulder. "Is that our sweet boy? I can't remember his name."

My heart dropped. Our? Did he remember Cooper? "Yes, it's Cooper, the Hipster."

"I loved that guy. We had some great times with him. Didn't we, Jilly Bean?"

Oh, my heavens! We? "Uh, yes. This guy really stole our hearts."

"He sure did. This painting makes me want another one. What do you think?"

My heart hammered. "I…I think we should look into it. There's nothing like the love of a sweet pup. Why don't we look at some adoption photos after dinner tonight?"

Chapter 36 Jill

The soft blue light of the TV and the flickering yellow of the fire cast dancing shadows across the walls of the den. Jim and I were settled on the couch enjoying movie night after our long day of gardening. The aroma of freshly-popped popcorn mingled with the sriracha we added as a topper. The smell was part of so many happy evenings enjoying each other's company, not just at home but when we used to have date night at the local theater, always keeping score of who owed who a movie. If I dragged him to a chick flick and he hated it, I'd have to sit through two action flicks. If I sat through one of his gruesome horror shows, he'd owe me two chick flicks. I popped a few kernels in my mouth. My tongue numbed as the spice soaked in. We'd cut down on salt years ago and always tossed our popcorn with a bit of the sriracha powder we used for our eggs. It was surprisingly delicious the first time we tried it, so we made it our go-to topper.

Tonight's movie was about a teacher who adopted one of her troubled students. It was one of my favorites because it brought back so many memories of my own experiences with students. So many of those young ones had faced challenges with unwavering resilience. I kept in touch with a few. Many had turned their lives around. I was so proud to have been a part of helping them achieve their goals.

Jim and were about an hour and a half into the film when my mind wandered to the new pup we could be adopting. After dinner, we'd looked at a few photos and decided to rescue a senior dog. It shattered my heart that there were so many to choose from. I never understood how people could abuse and abandon animals. He agreed we had too much on our plates to train a puppy and give it the attention and energy it needed. I'd promised we'd go to the local shelter in the morning.

My attention returned to the TV as the lead character broke into tears when her adopted son gave an acceptance speech at an award ceremony. He thanked her for being his teacher, mother and staunch supporter.

Tears welled and fell from my eyes. I was over the moon that Jim had remembered Cooper, but sad about all the abuse in the world. Not just how humans treated animals, but how we treated each other and our own children. Jim must have sensed my turmoil. He set the bowl on the end table and held my hand. "I know we never adopted any of these kids, but you did good by your students. You should be proud. I know I am."

I let out a gasp. "That's so sweet of you. I am proud of each and every one of them. I only wish I could have done more." I wanted to ask about his memories of our life together. However, I knew asking loaded questions like "Do you remember x?" could shut dementia patients down as the pressure to remember triggered anxiety and frustration. Instead, I shared one of my favorite success stories.

"Well, I was never the recipient of an acceptance speech, but I had my share of emotional thank-you's over the years."

"Tell me your… the one you liked," he said with a smile.

"It would have to be Mark. He was in and out of foster homes from the age of five. I think the year he was with me, he switched homes three times."

"Wow. Why'd they keep moving him around?"

"I don't think the agency was honest with the foster parents about what they were getting into or they picked parents who already had a houseful and couldn't give him the attention he needed."

"Did you help?"

"I hope so. He was special the moment I saw him. I had to put him under my wing."

"What made you know he was special?"

"I could tell he didn't want to behave the way he was behaving, but he didn't know how to change. No one believed he could change, so how on earth could he believe it was possible? You know what I mean?"

"Yes. So what did you do?"

"I gave him extra tutoring sessions and a ton of patience. Honestly, more than I thought I had in me at times. He really tested me. He had trust issues and used his anger as a defense mechanism, so I kept at it. It wasn't easy for either of us, but he never walked away and did everything I asked. He turned his grades around, which helped build his confidence. Then he started making friends and showing pride in his work. Mark started helping students who were struggling, and before long, they all looked up to him. My favorite part was when I saw him a few years after graduation and he told me he paid it forward. When I asked him what he meant he told me he was a guidance counselor at one of the toughest schools. Mark told me I'd changed his life, and it's what made him want to be a mentor for troubled teens. He loved helping change the trajectory of their lives, the way I helped him." I wiped a tear from my eyes. "I still get emotional every time I think about him."

Jim squeezed my hand. "You have the biggest heart."

"Thanks, babe. I'm excited about getting Cooper Junior. I kinda miss having my heart melt at the sight of puppy eyes and puppy kisses."

"How about we call him Mini-Coop?"

"It sounds like a car."

He laughed. "I know. That's why I thought of it. Funny right?"

"It is. Can you see us calling him in from the yard? Come on Mini-Coop, here, boy. The neighbors will wonder what the heck we are doing."

"They'll love it once they meet him. What time does the shelter open?"

"Eight o'clock. Do you want to call first to see if we need an appointment or just head over?"

Jim scratched his head. "That's awfully early. Let's get coffee on the way."

"That's a stroke of genius!"

Jim yawned. "I'm ready to hit the hay. You joining me?"

"I'll tuck you in, but I want to puppy-proof the house. I have a feeling we'll bring home a new family member to-morrow."

"I thought we weren't getting a puppy."

"We aren't, but you never know what you're getting with a rescue."

"Want me to help?"

"No, let's get you settled. I won't take long."

Chapter 37 Jill

After watching the movie last night I knew we had to adopt from the local shelter downtown as they had a policy of putting down strays if not adopted within two weeks. To my delight, Jim remembered the conversation the next morning, and even talked about what a great dog Cooper had been. When we got there, the pup we agreed on from the website was already adopted. Despite our disappointment, we remained determined to adopt and requested to see the pups nearing the end of their stay or prepping for their last meal. The receptionist knew exactly what we meant and didn't seem surprised by the request. She rotated her monitor so we could see the pups that fell into our category.

I gasped. There was an entire page of them, at least a dozen. As I listened to the anxious barks coming from behind the door, some whimpers, some howls, some deep echoing laments, I wanted to take them all. I looked at Jim, and he had the same horror on his face. I asked if she knew the history of any of them. She only knew none were chipped, and they either didn't have collars or their collars didn't have tags. No one called to claim them and they didn't match any lost pet notices.

All these guys needed us, but we could only pick one. We agreed at our age, if the pup got sick or injured and couldn't walk, we'd need a smaller pup we'd be able to easily lift and carry to the car. There was a small Jack Russell terrier that had the sweetest face and the saddest eyes. His ears were back and if the picture were a video, I was certain he'd be shaking. I asked if they could take him to the adoption room so we could play with him.

We made our way through the kennels to the back room. The air resonated with a chorus of different breeds.

Small and large dogs sent yips and yelps that reverberated off the walls. It was as though the dogs knew we weren't staff but were here on a mission to adopt one of them. They tried desperately to get our attention, jumping against their cages and wagging their tails like raised hands. Pick me, please pick me, please pick me. It was all I could do not to burst into tears. It made me wonder why the adoption room wasn't before the kennels. Maybe it was their way of ensuring people reached out to their friends to adopt as well. I knew I'd be making a few calls.

We waited in the room a few minutes before the staff brought him in. He walked in slowly and kept his tail tucked. Before I knew it, Jim was on his knees doing the play bow and wiggling his butt. I broke out laughing. The pup jumped and seemed to spring to life. He play bowed back and bunny hopped over to Jim, jumping and kissing on him. I joined in on the fun. It took about an hour to finish the paperwork. They told us he was around three based on his dental. He was neutered, so he'd been someone's pet once. They told us they also walked all the dogs in the cat area to see who was aggressive so they could note the file for any dual pet owners. He paid no attention to the cats, even when they hissed. We didn't have a cat, but that was good to know, since sometimes our neighbor's cat jumped the fence and hung out in our backyard.

We stopped off at a pet store near the house and bought him everything a stray could dream of —like Oliver Twist dreamed of porridge and a clean cot. He had a new bed, jacket, a dozen toys, a leash, as well as a fresh bag of high-grade food we'd mix with the kibble the shelter gave us until his tummy could handle the switch.

Even though he looked nothing like our sweet Cooper, we kept the name Mini-Coop in his honor. We stopped off at the local park to take him for a short walk. He didn't bark at the other dogs, just wagged his tail and kept sniffing around.

Why would anyone have turned this sweet pup in? I figured he may have escaped from someone's yard, but why hadn't they come looking for him in almost two weeks? I decided they didn't deserve him if they couldn't be bothered to look for him. But I reminded myself that life can sometimes take unexpected turns. What if I had passed away before Jim, and he had a dog when dementia came to claim him? *Judge not lest you be judged, Jill.*

We already had a pet door from our prior pups, and after tossing a few treats through it, our Mini-Coop was going in and out on his own. He ran so much, his little heart was beating out of his chest. I brought him in, and he drank his entire bowl of water. I set his bed next to Jim's recliner and started a load of laundry. By the time I made it back to the den, he was curled up on Jim's lap. They were both sound asleep. I tip-toed in, turned down the TV and left them to bond.

I didn't tell Jim, but the reason I hadn't gone to bed with him last night was because I wanted to run the idea of adding a pet to the mix by Vicky. I wasn't sure if having a new pup was a good idea with all we had going on with Jim. She clapped with glee and told me it was actually the best thing. She'd known for years that research showed pets improved mental and physical health of both the care partner and their loved one.

I asked why she didn't suggest we get a dog earlier, and she told me she'd never suggest it to anyone who wasn't thinking about it already because of the cost and time burden it could place on an already-taxed care partner, but if they were on board on their own, she was delighted.

She peppered a host of benefits at me like a shaker with a loose top. A pet helped release an automatic relaxation response and was great therapy for reducing anxiety. A furry friend could even help in the recall of memories. Petting an animal could reduce blood pressure. When people pet or cuddle their pets, their body releases endorphins, oxytocin, and dopamine. I was sold the moment Mini-Coop bounced over to Jim but had to admit Vicky cheering us on made me feel much better.

We also talked about Jim remembering Cooper when he saw my painting, his more frequent use of 'Jilly Bean', and remembering that I taught troubled teens. She told me she didn't want to get my hopes up but felt like it was something that might happen since the doctor recently took him off three of his blood pressure meds. Every month, his pressure improved when we started meditating and added breath work, and even better when we tossed the junk food we used to eat. The dietary improvements were helping me at least as much as Jim. At my annual physical, my blood pressure was normal and my cholesterol was lower. The doctor reduced the dosage of Jim's medications until he was officially off all meds. Whether I was on borrowed time or not, I needed to enjoy and embrace every minute.

Chapter 38 Jim

The little guy was curled up in his dog bed, watching me paint. The afternoon sun streamed in through the windows and turned his bed into a little hot pad. I took a deep breath in and exhaled as my brush completed the last stroke across the canvas. "What do you think, little guy? Does this silver-haired fellow look like me?"

His ears perked up and his head turned to the side as he watched me looking at the mirror on the closet door and then back at the self-portrait I'd just completed. "Not bad, if I say so myself." His tail thumped in agreement.

"Thanks, half-pint."

I still had the skills to capture me, at least outwardly. The wrinkles around my eyes and mouth were there. My unruly silver bedhead in the mirror didn't match the perfect, not-a-hair-out-of-place mane of the portrait. I'd somehow captured my weariness.

The first piece was simple and reflected what the world saw when this all started. No outward signs of dementia. I thought back to a few friends insisting I didn't have the disease because I was articulate and strong. They were certain that it had to be something else. Despite the test results, they felt a second or even third opinion would reveal a different diagnosis, one less devastating. They were well-meaning. My guess was they needed a diagnosis easier to accept and process, as well as for me to handle. Even I had my doubts in the beginning when I'd catch my image at the gym lifting weights. I was strong, healthy, and vital. How could my brain not be as fit?

I set the painting aside and replaced it with a blank canvas. It was time to capture the more challenging present-day Jim. Rocking back on my heels, I stared hard at the white canvas before me. The problem was, I didn't know how to add what I'd call the piece of the disease that was bringing me to my knees. Of course, the eyes would be the best place to capture the phase where I was aware my mind was collapsing. Where I was aware of what I'd lost and feared the inevitable losses to come. They were the windows to the soul. But how could I convey this? Or the forgetfulness? How do I show the inside of my brain? What would those strokes of turning myself inside out look like? How could I capture words that escaped me? Would painting images eventually replace words?

My decision to follow other artists with self-portraits documenting their decent into mental illness or dementia seemed daunting and beyond my capabilities. How on earth would I keep up progressive portraits? How would I be able to capture what it feels like to forget everyone around me when I won't even be aware I'd forgotten them? Maybe I was further along than I thought. Maybe I'd forgotten what I'd done to deserve this. Surely I'd done something. Or is that what everyone felt when dealt a blow they didn't have the strength for? *What doesn't kill you strengthens you?* Was that the saying? I was certainly going to die with it, not necessarily from it with all my other health issues. Would it strengthen me along the way? Would I still be able to ponder these kind of questions?

I sat on the edge of the bed and patted the comforter. The little guy jumped next to me, and I scratched his head, then rubbed his shoulders. "I'm getting pretty darn dark, little buddy." He licked my chin and neck. His kisses tickled, and I laughed and picked him up for a hug. "Thanks, little dude. I needed that."

I held him in my arms and walked over to Jill's portrait of our old pup. "You'd have loved our … sweet… sweet….Coo…Cooper. He was a good pup. Just like you…

Mini-Coop." My mood shifted. "Little dude, I'm going to paint your first portrait." I sat him down, cranked up the music, and let the joy I felt move my brush. I wasn't that far along and had plenty of time to do my next self-portrait.

I started by drawing out the shape of his head. I looked at Jill's portrait and down at the little guy back in his bed. Although he was much smaller, his forehead was much broader before it tapered to a blunt muzzle. I outlined his furry head cocked to one side like he had it when he watched me looking at my image. I wasn't sure if I'd be able to capture his beautiful, soulful eyes, but I gave it my best shot. They were harder to paint than when I used to sketch eyes. I filled the round shapes with brown and black dots, then added a spot of white I'd hoped would make it look like light hitting his eyes, but it seemed too bright. I wasn't happy with it, but moved on before I got frustrated and ruined it tinkering too much. I figured I could always go back and touch it up later. The thick, textured brush-strokes I used to build the layers of fur didn't come out right either, so I added a few dashes of white to add high-lights across his coat. I added some black for his nose and red for his tongue. He looked like a cartoon. I was rushing and shouldn't have started by trying to draw it out with a paintbrush. Clearly, I didn't have the skills to eyeball it. I looked around for my old tool box of supplies Jill brought to our studio. I should have started with a light pencil like Shirley. It was next to the bed!

I set the canvas against the wall to dry and put up a new blank one. "Sorry, Mini-Coop, for a cartoon painting. It's not bad. It's just as cute as you in a goofy way. For your first portrait, though, let's do it right. What do you think, buddy?"

Mini-Coop thumped his tail and snapped to attention.

"Stretch break?"

His tail thumping doubled in speed.

"I'm totally on board with that! How about a stretch, snack, and then we get right back at it?"

Chapter 39 Jill

It had been a few weeks since we brought the Mini-Coop home. It was as if he was channeling our old pup. He followed Jim around just like Cooper. But instead of calling him the Hipster, I called him the Kneester since he barely reached Jim's knees. Jim was in the backyard throwing a ball to tire him out before we headed to the Memory Café. Vicky let us bring him to our weekly sessions to help develop his canine social skills and give anyone who didn't have a pet the opportunity to love on him. He was a ham who liked to be the center of attention, accepted love from all directions, and collected hearts along the way. His most endearing trait was the way he backed up to get his shoulders rubbed. When the giver of such rubbing stopped, he'd bring his head back and look at them with the sweetest eyes like, "You're not done, are you?" He played that con on everyone in the circle. They all expected it, but burst out laughing when it was their turn.

We decided not to bring him today. Apparently, there was going to be a special talk from one of the member's sons and we thought Mini-Coop might be too big of a distraction. The upcoming session was all mysterious. We were told to bring paintings we'd completed. Things had been a bit hectic, so our only submissions were the two we painted with the group, plus Jim's self-portrait and my portrait of Cooper. At least we'd finished those.

I got our paintings loaded in the car and stuffed a toy with a dog treat to keep the Kneester busy. I put up a pet gate to keep him in the kitchen near his pet door/escape hatch. He hadn't shown any signs of destructive behavior, but I knew we'd be gone for a few hours and we had never left him for more than an hour. I had plenty of experience coming home to the antics of a bored dog. I waved to Jim through the window and they both came barreling in, hot with excitement and out of breath.

I hydrated them both—a few ice cubes in Mini-Coop's bowl and poured a glass of cool filtered ice water for Jim. "Have a seat and finish this. You're going to wear yourself out."

"He's a little toot that one."

"Well, you're a big toot, so I guess you two are a match made in heaven."

Jim laughed and finished his water.

I grabbed his glass and placed it in the sink. "We'd better get going."

"Are we bringing the little guy?"

Jim had trouble remembering his name, so he just called him the little guy. I'm sure it was my fault because I constantly switched between nicknames like "Kneester," "Mini," and "Super-Duper-Cooper." I kept making a mental note to stick to one but was so used to doing that with our big Cooper. "No, that's why I had you throw the ball. Marg's son is going to give a special talk today, and our boy here is such a scene-stealer no one will pay attention to her son."

"Which son?"

"The neurologist."

"Is he looking for Guinea pigs for a study or looking to get new clients? He's got a room full to pick from." He laughed.

"I doubt it. She said he was very successful and renowned in his field."

"Have you met him?"

"No, but she's really good about sharing anything from his studies that can help us. He's why we changed our diet and how we exercise."

"How we exercise?"

"You know how we added all that cross midline stuff to engage both sides of the brain? Like touching your right arm to your left knee and then your left arm to your right knee."

"I did that when I was a kid. He didn't make that up."

"He didn't say he made it up. He said he thought it was helpful to wake up the brain."

Jim stood up and did a few and knocked on his head. "No kidding. Wakey, wakey, brain."

"Oh, my heavens, you're a nut. Grab your coat. We've got to get going." I chuckled.

"Are we bringing the little guy?"

"Uh, no, sorry"

"Why? They love him."

For time constraints, I went with a shorter explanation. "We've got to get him used to us being gone for longer than an hour. Now give him a good scratch and we've got to get going."

Chapter 40 Jill

I thought we'd be the first ones at the support group, but almost everyone was already there setting up their canvases. Jim had a painting in each hand, as did I. We made our way to an open area where we could set up our easels side-by-side. There was a diffuser in the corner, sending bursts of lavender essential oil into the air every few minutes. I breathed in the calming aroma as Jim placed our paintings on the open easels.

Once again, the room was transformed into an art studio. The sunlight from the windows illuminated the kaleidoscope of colors, adding warmth to the vibrant hues. This time, our little studio was much more magnificent than our first paint and munch event, as we had triple the paintings since then. We walked around to admire everyone's work. The energy was palpable with giddy excitement as we took turns examining each other's paintings. We had all poured our souls onto our canvases. The emotions expressed with each brushstroke made sense as we learned the stories behind them.

I stood in front of William's canvas and put my hand over my heart. "William, it's beautiful. You really captured the waves striking the large rock. I had no idea you were so talented. It takes my breath away."

"I'll admit, Shirley's sketch guided me. It's Cannon Beach in Oregon, where Sally and I spent our honeymoon. It's one of our favorite vacation spots. I almost got knocked off the rocks by a wave while taking the photo, but it was worth it."

"What a beautiful sunset to contrast the blue water and whitecaps!"

"The entire week was magical, with the most beautiful sunsets," Sally added.

I looked at her canvas. She had a different image of her beagle pup from the one she painted during our event. "Is that Max? I love it. He looks so cute holding the donut toy in his mouth. I love the way it frames his face, like he's peeking through a round window."

"You remember his name! Yes, that's our Max. He loved that toy."

"You captured him even better than the first one. You're getting really good at this."

"I've got the same confession. The foundation was Shirley's sketch."

"But you still did a beautiful job. I'm using her sketch, too. You inspired me with Max, so I painted our old pup, Cooper. Come see ours. Jim's is a self-portrait." We were almost in front of our canvases when Janet gave a low whistle.

"I know everyone is enjoying these beautiful works of art. I promise we will have time to share after the lecture. Everyone take their seats, please. The Richardsons' son, David, just arrived. We're about to get started."

Our guest speakers rarely used a podium. They usually sat in the circle of chairs with us. This time, the chairs were arranged in more formal rows with empty spaces at the end of the row to accommodate wheelchairs. We took the two chairs to the right of William and Sally, and Shirley sat next to Jim. I asked Jim to switch seats as I hadn't had the chance to catch up with her. I leaned in and gave her a hug before sitting down. "This is all so mysterious. We usually get a full agenda of guest speakers. Do you know what this is about?"

"I do." She giggled. "You'll know in just a minute. It's going to blow your mind."

A strikingly handsome man in his forties made his way to the podium with a laptop and folders cradled in his arm. He had a gorgeous head of wavy chestnut hair, contrasting with all the thinning silver or balding heads in the room. He wore a casual brown jacket over a blue shirt and gray slacks. I could see Marg and her husband, Jack in his countenance. Janet was already standing at the podium, ready to introduce him. He placed his items in the center of the lectern and gave Janet a hug and a kiss on the cheek.

Janet lifted the mic from the stand. "Hello, everyone. I think a few of you already know this distinguished gentleman standing next to me. Not only is he a very dear friend, he's the son of Marg and Jack Richardson. It's our good fortune that he is a renowned neurologist, and since his dad's diagnosis a few years ago, he's made it his mission to focus his practice and attention on helping those diagnosed with dementia. Please give David a warm round of applause."

The room erupted with claps and whistles. Those who could easily stand, stood. He smiled and held his hands up and motioned for us to sit.

"I'm honored to receive such a warm welcome."

One of the center's employees set up Jack's painting on an easel next to him. He had captured a breathtaking scene of rolling green hills and a crystal-clear lake surrounded by trees dotted with autumn colors of orange, yellow, and rustic brown. He moved next to the painting and took a moment to admire it. His voice choked when he began.

"Dad hadn't touched a paintbrush in ten years before this painting. His prior paintings hung in galleries across the state and each one sold for thousands." He walked back to the lectern and held tight to the sides.

"Some of you are new to this creative outlet, having first experienced its power to awaken memories and evoke emotions during your paint-and-dine experience." A few heads nodded.

"Raise your hands if this is the first time you've worked with a canvas."

More hands raised than not.

"Would anyone care to share their experience?"

Only a few hands dropped. He picked Sally.

"I'm the care partner, but my memory isn't the greatest these days either. When I painted my sweet Max, I started remembering all the good times we had with our little fur baby. And, well, all of his destructive antics as well, which at the time weren't funny, but now I can't stop laughing when I share the stories of all the shoes he ate."

"Beautiful. Thank you for sharing. It really does have the power to awaken memories and evoke emotions. How many of you noticed that, especially since you were working from photos of your own experiences?"

Almost everyone raised their hands. The few that couldn't nodded.

"Dad experienced the same thing. Even more remarkable, I saw him come more alive these past few months with each masterpiece he finished. He had tapped into something that the family believed would be dormant forever. We never thought to ask him to paint again. His arthritis was so painful, and he had difficulty with focus. Yet, it was as if the movement was oil for his joints and the detail needed for the image held his focus." He motioned to Jack's painting. "He couldn't paint for hours on end like he used to, but moment by moment, this beautiful piece emerged."

He opened a folder and removed a piece of paper. "I didn't come here to brag about Dad's painting. When I saw the difference in him after painting again, just like I saw him come alive with music therapy, I had to see what combining the two could do. In the past, he always played music when he created his art. With this piece here, we played his favorite music. We compared the painting to your first painting event, and given that he'd been out of practice when he painted that day, there wasn't just a difference in the two paintings, there was a difference in his symptoms. Without using technical jargon, I'll try to explain."

"Perhaps I should tell you the good news first. Would you like to hear it or wait until the end?"

Everyone chanted, "Good News!"

He laughed. "Alright, then, good news it is! When I saw the difference in Dad and Mom, I did some research and saw documented research that both music and creative exercises had a positive impact on both dementia patients and their care partners. I knew what areas of the brain were engaged with each and realized when you combine the two, you fuse both your auditory and visual senses, blending the two into a unique sensory experience. The emotions evoked by the music and even the rhythm of the piece selected influence the brushstrokes. Creativity uses a different part of the brain than verbal responses and offers an opportunity to tap into and share memories and emotion without the pressure of using words. The rhythm, melody, and emotions conveyed by the music guide the brush stroke, allowing the inner creativity to flourish. It's not about creating a masterpiece; it's about expressing yourself freely, without judgment or limitations. Janet shared she wanted to submit her program for grants, and I volunteered to take that on. The good news is I received a five-year grant to study the two mediums combined and am here today to ask if I can follow your progress for my research."

We looked at each other with wide amazement. Was our work worthy of such a contribution? I realized the end result wasn't the final painting; it was the process. I yelled out, "I'm in."

There was a chorus of "Me, too, I'm in."

"Thank you. I'm honored. I'd like to share at a high level what's going on in the brain. The moment you pick up the brush and stare at that canvas, whether blank or beautifully outlined with Shirley's sketch, several areas of your brain are firing. The visual cortex engages, helping you process the colors and shapes of your masterpiece. As you move the brush across the canvas, the area responsible for motor skills kicks in, helping you guide your brushstrokes. And as most of you have already discovered, your emotional processing centers switch on with your creative choices. That's without music. Throw music in the mix and now you've activated the auditory areas of the brain. When you harmonize the two, your brain forms neural pathways that intersect and connect. How powerful is that?"

Everyone clapped.

"As you repeat the behavior, areas that fire together wire together. My hypothesis is that if you listen to familiar, emotionally-triggering music while painting, it will help retrieve memories or at least deep-seated emotions from your limbic system. This is the area of the brain that controls emotions. Not only will it enhance the creative process, it will blend the emotions and recollections which, I believe, will strengthen cognitive function, help with emotional behaviors, and don't get me started on the social benefits gained from doing this project as a group. That's a research grant all on its own." He looked around the room. "Does anyone have any questions?"

Shirley raised her hand and blurted out. "Thank you for doing this. We owe you!"

"You don't owe me. It's the other way around. But if you feel that way, there is a way you can pay it forward. I think we can use your stories and paintings in an exhibit to educate the community. I'd love it if each of you could stand or sit in front of your paintings and share your experience while painting and why you selected that image. We've got one more treat. Before you head to your canvases, Janet has some more exciting news."

Janet stepped next to him. "Thank you, David. We are organizing a community outreach in a few months and are hoping each of you will show your paintings and talk about any changes you've noticed since joining the music and art therapy program. We will use the proceeds from the event tickets to continue the program and help families in need."

Jim stood and cleared his throat. "I'd be honored to donate a painting to auction if you think it will help. This program has given us so much. It's the least I can do to give back."

There was another chorus of "Me, too" and "I'm in."

Janet brought her hands to her chest. "Thank you all so much. Just one painting each. Your work is a legacy for you and your family to keep. This is going to be the best event! I'll keep you posted as we get closer. In the meantime, I've set up a table with delicious sandwiches and snacks. I thank you for your time. David and I look forward to speaking to each of you about your paintings."

We headed over to the feast of goodies. The room echoed with everyone's chatter and laughter.

Chapter 41 Jill

The months flew by as Jim and I threw ourselves into painting. The grant had given us a newfound sense of purpose, and we were determined to make the most of it. As the weeks turned into months, painting became as natural as breathing, a part of our weekly routine that brought us closer. I had hoped to establish a daily practice, but we definitely had something competing for our time. Everything we did revolved around our sweet Mini-Coop. Although he was a good pup from the beginning, he needed some additional training.

Since we were taking him to the center every week, we had to break him of his habit of jumping on everyone. Almost all the members had thin skin because of age, and most had balance issues. Not the best combination for sudden jumps and nails raking across their legs. He had graduated from his training class with honors and was the perfect pet and mascot for the center. Everyone loved him and looked forward to playing with him during our weekly sessions.

I felt him stir against my leg and slowly opened my eyes. I didn't want to wake Jim, so I lifted the covers and whispered, "Good morning, little guy."

He made his way to the top of the covers and gave me kisses on my cheek. This was our first small dog, and we were adjusting to the different behaviors of his breed. For one, he loved to be covered and insisted on sleeping under the blanket and absolutely had to have body contact. Although he and Jim were inseparable by day, he chose me to sleep next to. Our prior pups were too large for the bed, so it was an adjustment to have him sleep with us. At first, I had a hard time sleeping, but soon his fur was comforting, and I was out like a light.

A strong, not quite smell of wet dog made its way into my nostrils. "Mini-Coop, what have you been rolling in?" I buried my nose in his fur. It smelled just fine. "Is that your breath, buddy? What the heck have you been eating?" I took a closer smell of his breath. Not ideal, but that wasn't the smell either.

Jim stirred at our activity and opened his eyes. Mini-Coop bounced on his chest and gave him kisses. Jim laughed. "Good morning, little guy. You ready to go outside?"

Mini-Coop jumped down from the bed and turned in circles, ending in a few front hops. Something our larger pups never did, and it made me laugh every time. Except now, the smell coming from Jim distracted me.

"Babe, I don't know how else to say this, but you're ripe. What the heck did you do yesterday?"

"Ripe? What?"

"Let's just say you don't smell like a bed of roses. Why don't you hop in the shower, and I'll let our little guy out and feed him?"

Jim groaned. "I don't smell. It's the little guy. He toots under the covers all night."

"Um, I gave him the sniff test. It's you. Sorry, babe. Just take a quick shower and I'll take care of the pup and start the coffee." I stood and started to walk out of the bedroom when I looked back at Jim. He stood at the doorway of the bathroom, frozen.

"Babe, everything okay?"

"I can't remember how to make the water fall."

"The water fall? The shower. Oh, that's okay, hon. I'll get it started for you." I hadn't realized he had been skipping his daily shower.

He followed me to the bathroom. I turned it on, and, when the temperature was just right, I dried my hand. He felt the water, stepped back, and hesitated.

"Jim, what's wrong? Is it too hot?"

"I don't like it hitting my face."

"You don't have to face the water. You can turn around and let it hit the back of your head."

"I don't need a shower."

I was prepared for this. It was something several members at the support group talked about over the past year. I tried to remember the solutions offered. Always give options. We could just wash up in the sink. Maybe that could be plan B. First, I'd try the shower. "We can make it a spa day. I can light a candle and draw a bath. Would you like a bath or shower?"

"Baths are for girls. A shower, but I don't want my face wet."

"The shower head removes. How about you step in, and you can draw the shower curtain for privacy? I'll reach around and hand you the shower head or I can do it for you. I'll look away. You can guide my hand if you want."

"I don't need a shower."

Plan B. "Um. You know, Shirley's husband has been raving about this new soap. She gave me a sample. Let me get it. I bet you'll love it. It's a liquid, so it will work better in the shower. Would you like to try it and I'll use the shower head to make sure your face doesn't get wet?" I needed to give him a task. "Why don't you start unbuttoning your PJs while I grab the sample?"

I stepped away and looked around, as though deep in thought about where I put the sample. "Go ahead and step in the shower if you get your PJs off before I get back." I grabbed a new soap from the hall closet and opened the pet door for Mini-Coop. When I walked back in, Jim was in the shower with the curtain drawn.

I wet a washcloth and added the soap. "I'm going to reach my hand in the curtain and hand you the wash cloth. It smells very manly. I think you'll love it." I felt Jim take it from my hand.

"Do you need help?"

"Can you pull down the sprayer?"

"Of course." I reached in and pulled it down, aiming the spray at the floor so it wouldn't splash his face. "Here you go." I could hear him moving and washing.

"I'm done."

"We're going to need to wash your hair, or at least get it wet. I can do that for you to make sure your face doesn't get wet. Would you like that?"

"Yes."

I leaned in and let the water fall gently on his hair. "How about I massage your head with some shampoo, or would you like to do it?"

"You can."

I put a small amount in one hand and held the sprayer with the other. I put the shampoo on his hair and realized I needed both hands. "Can you hold the sprayer while I massage the shampoo in?"

He didn't answer but grabbed the sprayer and aimed it at his feet. He leaned his head back, enjoying the massage.

"Can you hand me the sprayer? I'm going to slowly rinse the shampoo out of your hair. I like the way you are leaning back a bit. It'll help me from getting it in your face."

I rinsed his hair, turned the water off, and handed him a towel. "All good and squeaky clean?"

He dried himself with the curtain closed, wrapped the towel around his waist, then pulled the curtain back. "Thank you."

"You're welcome. I laid your sweatshirt and sweatpants on the bed with clean undergarments. Why don't you get dressed and I'll start the coffee?"

He didn't answer but nodded and walked toward the bed. Shirley and I had our weekly get together this afternoon. I wondered if she had similar problems with her husband Carl and how quickly he progressed after this stage. I was also grateful Vicky would spend the afternoon with Jim. She'd be able to gauge his progress and we could discuss it when I got back from lunch. Between Shirley and Vicky, I'd have a better idea of this new stage we had entered.

Chapter 42 Jill

Shirley met me in the lobby area of the retirement community's main campus. I gave her a hug.

"Holy cow. It's beautiful in here. It's so warm and welcoming," I said.

"Isn't it?!"

We walked over to the receptionist's desk and signed in. The large, polished wooden counter was the central focal point of the lobby. A receptionist who had to be in her seventies greeted us. I imagined she was one of the residents, excited by the opportunity to be of service to the community. She turned the sign-in sheet toward her so she could read our names and who we were here to visit. "Good afternoon, ladies. I'll let Anna know you are here." She pushed an intercom button on her phone. "Your guests have arrived."

A soft voice came through the speaker. "Lovely, I'll be right down."

The receptionist smiled and motioned to a nearby seating area. "It will just be a minute. You're welcome to have a seat."

Shirley returned the welcoming smile. "Thanks. Have a great day."

"You as well." She turned to answer the ringing phone.

We made our way over to the cozy upholstered chairs and sofa. Shirley pointed to the beautifully framed photographs and artwork on the surrounding wall. "They have an art studio here. The residents created most of the artwork. It's a gorgeous studio. That and the salt water pool sold me."

I felt the leaves of the plant resting on a three-legged table between our two chairs. "These indoor plants are gorgeous and so healthy. Someone here has a green thumb."

"Maybe my plants will stand a chance here. I wonder if they take care of the plants in the villas."

"Villa?"

"It's the name they call the section of single-family homes."

"Sounds fancy."

"It does sound better than old-age home." She laughed. "We have a weekly maid service. Maybe they take care of the plants as well."

"Maid service. We might just get a place next to you!"

"Wouldn't that be perfect?"

Shirley stood and grabbed a few brochures from a well-organized rack showcasing newsletters and brochures. Then she walked over to a nearby bulletin board displaying notices and announcements of the latest happenings within the community. "There are a ton of activities here. We won't be bored."

"This sounds like a slice of heaven."

"Hello, ladies. I'm so sorry I took so long."

We turned to the sweet voice we'd heard on the intercom. Shirley extended her hand to Anna, the social events coordinator. "Thanks for giving me a second tour. It's good to see you again."

Anna returned the handshake. "It's my pleasure and thank you for bringing a guest." She turned to me and shook my hand with a firm but quick pump. "It's a pleasure to meet you, Mrs. Bish. I'm here to answer any questions you may have."

She had a young person's enthusiasm and bounce to her step. Her jet-black hair was cut in a stylish shag. Her uniform hugged her athletic frame. She handed each of us our badges.

"Here you go, Mrs. Bish."

"Please, Jill. Mrs. Bish makes me feel old. Well, older than I am."

"Pleasure to meet you, Jill." She looked at Shirley's hand holding the brochures. "You'll see in that brochure there is no shortage of activities here."

"I saw the bulletin board as well. You've got about every interest for your residents covered," Shirley said.

"Does that include photography?" I asked.

Anna clapped. "It does! We even have classes for our residents on how to take stunning photos with their phones. I take it you're a photographer."

"An amateur, but I love it and wouldn't mind taking that class one day. This place is amazing. Shirley told me about the tiered living and care. It sounds like a perfect set-up to age into."

"It is. I believe it will leave quite an impression on you. Shall we make our way to the dining hall?"

Shirley motioned for Anna to lead the way. "I'm starving."

"Wonderful. Our executive chef, sous chef, and senior chef have extensive experience either owning or working in five-star restaurants."

"Wow, why are there so many chefs?" I asked.

"They each have an important role in the hierarchy. The executive chef, Kathy, oversees the daily operations of the kitchen, food prep and menu planning. She creates almost all the recipes. Her sous chef runs the kitchen when she can't be there and oversees the details of each dish. The senior chef is the station chef who excels in dishes required by some of the unique dietary needs of a few residents."

She activated a door with her badge. "Please tap each of your badges on the security panel. It helps monitor where our residents and guests are. Of course, residents can hold the door open for someone behind them or with them, but we have a strict policy that everyone's badge must be scanned by the card reader before entering any of the areas."

Shirley laughed. "Feels a bit like Fort Knox."

"It's necessary to account for everyone's whereabouts. Should there be a need to evacuate the building, the staff knows exactly where everyone is to make sure the building is cleared quickly and safely."

"Makes sense." Shirley nodded.

Anna guided us down a long hall lined with residents' apartment doors. "This is the assisted living area."

The residents individually decorated their doors with unique items. Some placed chairs and a small table for socializing near their door. All had a dry erase board with information about the resident to include their likes and favorite hobbies to assist with talking points when greeting the resident. The doors also had a side window with lace curtains.

"I like the window. It's a nice touch," I said.

"It lets the residents see who is knocking at their door before opening, and some don't care to sit in their simulated 'front porch' area but instead prefer to look out the side glass as residents and staff pass by."

We waved to a few residents as we made our way to the dining area. An elderly female in a purple sweatsuit waved at us from her swinging chair. Her poodle was sound asleep next to her.

"Here we are." The dining area was at the dead end of the hallway. There was no door to activate. The design was an open setting of several hundred tables. The area was alive with chatter and staff attending to the tables.

"Because all our residents use the dining area, including those in the memory care center, couples that have separate living environments can still enjoy each other's company in the dining and social areas. Shirley, I forgot to ask, will Carl be joining us?"

"It's just us gals. I'll be having dinner with him tonight."

"How delightful, a girls' day. One of the beautiful things about living in this community is the cherished friendships you will build. Socializing is critical and something we make easy with all our activities."

"I'm finding that to be true. I'm able to handle the stress of being thrust into the role of care partner so much easier since joining the support group and becoming friends with this amazing lady." I pointed to Shirley.

Shirley blushed. "Aw. Right back at you."

"I'm glad you two found each other." Anna sat us at a table and motioned for two ladies talking in the corner to join us.

"As we approached the table, she raised her voice a bit and introduced them as Nancy and Freda. Nancy was stout with a cute cardigan over her T-shirt. Freda was the taller of the two and greeted us with a grin. After introducing Shirley and me, Anna said, "Nancy and Freda are long-term-residents and ambassadors of our community. I've asked them to join you two for lunch so you can get a first-hand account of life here at the center. I hope you don't mind."

"Not at all. Thank you for arranging this," Shirley said.

"I need to get back to the office. Please reach out to me if you need anything or have any questions. You ladies enjoy yourselves."

I smiled. "Thank you. It was so nice to meet you. I'm sure I'll be reaching out soon."

"I look forward to it."

I tried not to stare, but Nancy looked too young to be a resident. She pinned her strawberry hair high in a bun, with not a gray strand in sight. She had the kind of face that seemed to defy age, with only a few fine lines around her eyes hinting at the wisdom of her years.

"I'm hoping you'll take this as a compliment, but aren't you too young to live here?"

She patted my hand. "That's the sweetest thing to say. It's true." She laughed. "But still the sweetest thing to say. I've got a house in the villa. My husband was in a terrible auto accident with extensive brain injuries. It happened five years ago. Unfortunately, he's had several strokes on top of that. He's in his sixties now and living in the full-time care section of the development. He can't join me for meals, but I visit him several times a day."

"You didn't want to stay in your old home?"

"Heavens, no. It was a five-bedroom home on an acre and way too much for one person to handle. He had always been the one to take care of the yard. Besides, it was a forty-five-minute drive each way. I was worn out running back and forth. Honestly, I've had much more of a social life since moving here than I did my forty years of marriage. Richard and I were joined at the hip and really only hung around each other."

Shirley nodded. "I get that. Since my Carl and I retired, it was just the two of us until we joined the support group."

"I noticed after Jim's diagnosis, friends and coworkers stopped coming by. The same goes for us; until we joined the Memory Café, it was just the two of us. One thing I'm learning through all of this, even if you're healthy, you've got to have friends and a community support system. Aging takes a toll, and aging with health issues, well, you just can't do it alone," I said.

Freda held her hands high. "Amen, sister." She was simply charming. Her gray hair had speckles of black and her blue eyes sparkled when she laughed.

The staff came over and took our orders. I ordered a salmon salad, and Shirley picked a steak and baked potato. Freda and Nancy ordered shrimp pasta. We waited until the server filled our water glasses to start asking questions.

"So, what's your favorite part about living here?" I asked.

Freda was the first to chime in. "I love game night."

Nancy nodded. "Sure, that's fun. But I love the gym and pool. They've got water aerobics four times a week."

"I'd love to join water aerobics," I said.

"You know what else I love?" Freda asked.

"No. What?" Shirley asked.

"I love karaoke on Friday nights."

Shirley and I looked at each other. Music and art. This really was the perfect place. I pointed to Shirley. "We both love music and art. So do our husbands."

Freda leaned in. "Speaking of husbands, since you two are married, I'll just tell you up front, the women outnumber the men here, as you can see. Hold on to your men tight. These ladies are like vultures when a new man moves in. They don't care if he's married or not."

Nancy admonished her. "Oh, don't go scaring them off. It's not like they rip their clothes off or anything. It's just they get lonely, and it's nice to have attention every now and again."

Shirley grabbed a bread roll and buttered it. "If they want my Carl, they'll have to change his diaper."

Freda turned red. "Okay, he's safe."

I laughed. "She's pulling your leg."

Shirley shook her head. "No, I'm not. That's why we're here. I love the man, but he's over 200 pounds. I just couldn't take care of him. It was killing my back."

I thought of Jim and knew not everyone hit this stage, but it was a possibility. Shirley must have seen my face drop because she changed the subject.

"They haven't given me the keys to my house yet. They're remodeling it. It's standard procedure every ten years. The person who moved out lived there for eleven years. I'm getting new paint, flooring, counters, the works. What do you say we take a walk after lunch and take a peek through the windows?"

"I'd love to see it," I said.

"Are we invited?" Freda asked.

Shirley nodded. "Sure. Why not? The more, the merrier."

Chapter 43 Jill

The property had beautiful walking trails that wound through small one-story homes spread over 300 acres. Of course, the sidewalks were smooth and even. They had to be well maintained, no broken hips on their watch. Each of the homes had manicured lawns and lovely flowerbeds. A few of the homes had small picket fences for owners with pets.

On the right side of the property, small rolling hills housed the residents' exclusive golf course. The greens were so neat and perfect it looked like miles of velvet green carpet. The fairways further encouraged an active lifestyle.

Shirley shared she was renting Sally Freeman's place since she'd transferred to the assisted living apartment. Freda and Nancy knew her well and took the lead. They were arm in arm, chatting and giggling like schoolgirls. I wasn't sure if they locked arms because they were such dear friends or if it was to keep Freda from falling. She had to be in her nineties. She had spunk, though, that was for sure. It was almost a mile before we made it to Shirley's house. I had stuffed myself with the most delicious meal I had in months and welcomed the walk.

Shirley's home was at the end of a cul-de-sac, giving her a larger yard than the homes along the main drag. The outside had already received a fresh coat of paint. Black shutters stood in sharp contrast with the white stucco walls.

There was a construction van out front and several work horses and electric tools strewn about the driveway and front yard. The work crew must have taken a lunch break because no one was on site. The garage was open, but the interior garage door was locked, so we walked around and looked in each of the windows.

"Oh, my word, they're so far along. The floors are already done," Shirley exclaimed.

I cupped my hands around my eyes and peered in at the hardwood floors. "They're gorgeous."

Freda and Nancy pressed their hands against the window and expressed their oohs and aahs.

Shirley turned on her heels. "Let's head to the kitchen."

We followed her to the side of the house. She did a little dance. "The counters are in, and they painted the walls already!"

Freda and Nancy leaned into the window. "That's a gorgeous soft green," Freda said.

"It sure is," Nancy agreed.

I looked in. "I love that center island. This place is beautiful. When do you think you can move in?"

"They said a month, but they're really plugging along. Maybe sooner."

"Jim and I better get over to your place and get you boxed up."

"I'd appreciate that."

Freda saw two friends walking on the trail. "Ladies, it was a pleasure meeting you both. I can't wait to see you guys again. Welcome to the community. I'm going to catch up with my friends and work off my lunch. Nancy, want to join me?"

"I'd be delighted. These hips need a few more steps as well." She turned and gave both of us a hug. "I can't wait to see more of you two. You take care now and let me know if you need help getting settled."

We said simultaneously, "Thanks. It was nice meeting you."

They waved and headed down the trail.

Shirley turned back to the window. "They sure are nice. It's great to get a proper welcome from ambassadors to the community."

"I think you're going to love it here."

"Are you thinking of joining me?"

My voice dropped. "It might be sooner than I expected. Can I ask if Carl forgot how to run the shower? I didn't realize Jim wasn't showering because he couldn't turn the water on."

Shirley nodded. Her smile faded. "Yes. That happened to Carl as well, and he didn't tell me either. I felt horrible because I used his not showering as punishment."

"What do you mean?"

"When he refused to shower, I told him he couldn't go to the Memory Café. I knew how much he loved it and figured it would motivate him. It took him two weeks of missing it before he admitted he didn't know how to work the shower knobs. I felt so horrible. I broke down in tears."

"Oh my. Can I ask how fast he progressed after that?"

"No, you may not. Everyone progresses at different speeds. Don't start jumping ahead."

I sobbed. She reached over and hugged me. "It's okay. Let it out."

I clung to her. "It's just Jim's been following the same protocol and diet changes Carl has, and Carl...."

She held me by the shoulders and looked me in the eye; her face was soft and compassionate. "I know, and Carl's hit a rapid decline. Carl's got other health issues, you can't compare. Even if Jim had the same health issues, you can't compare. This is an individual journey. You know that from seeing everyone's stages in the group. Jim could stay at that stage for ten years or... not."

I nodded, sniffling, comforted by her words. "I know you're right. Sorry, I didn't mean to dampen the excitement of your new home."

"Don't be silly. I'm always here for you. Want to see the backyard and check out the master bedroom? It's small, but it does have a nice walk-in closet."

We made our way to the back yard. There was a small pond nearby. "You've got a lake view. I'd never leave my back porch."

"It's more like a retention pond, but I'll pretend it's a lake. I can't wait to move in."

"When's the housewarming party?"

"As soon as I can get everything unpacked and organized."

Chapter 44 Jill

I walked into the kitchen and heard Vicky and Jim laughing. Vicky had soft jazz playing in the background. They each held a piece of puzzle in their hand, hovering it over where they thought it should land. Mini-Coop was sleeping under the table. I set my purse down on the counter and stood next to Jim's chair and peered over his shoulder.

The border of the puzzle was complete, as was most of the top. I looked at the lid. The puzzle was of a horse race —maybe the Kentucky Derby—as a few ladies in the stands wore colorful hats.

"Hi, guys. What's so funny?"

Vicky was still giggling when she tried to share the details. "Hi. Jim.... Jim.. When he... When he. haa haa haa. You tell it Jim, haa haa."

Jim grinned. "Mom and Dad used to take us horseback riding on the weekends. One weekend, we rented our horses too close to dinner. We were about twenty minutes away from the barn just doing a slow four-beat walk. Dad was pointing out the names of the trees and Mom was telling us the names of the birds. That's what we always did. Well... this time...." Jim's shoulders shook. He drew his head back and couldn't stop laughing. He put his hands over his belly.

Vicky burst into laughter and slapped her leg. They wiped tears from their eyes.

I laughed with them. "I have no idea why I'm laughing. What happened?"

They settled down. Jim continued. "It was the craziest thing. We had about ten minutes before we were supposed to turn around. But all of a sudden, all four horses at the exact same time turned around and took off in a full run back to the barn. I mean, it was like we were on race horses. None of us could control them, no matter how hard we pulled on the reins."

He slapped his leg. "Dad almost got knocked off his horse by a low-hanging branch, so we all laid down against our horses and held on to the western saddle horn for dear life. Then, when we got back to the barn, each horse stopped so hard we almost flew off. Turns out it was their dinner time, and they had no intention of being late."

We all broke out laughing again.

"We made sure we never rented before breakfast or dinner after that."

"That must have been scary. How old were you?"

"Maybe ten. Ella had been taking lessons on the English saddle, so she insisted on using one for the trail. We had no idea how she stayed on. Grace of God, really."

"Wow. So glad you guys weren't hurt. I'm surprised you weren't afraid to ride after that. I think I would've been."

"Nah, we knew why they did it. We just made sure they had a full belly for future rides."

I looked at the puzzle. "Do you guys want help with that? Or, since it's almost dinner time, I can make us some grilled cheese sandwiches and tomato soup?"

Vicky perked up. "I was going to head out, but Jim told me you really are a master of the grilled cheese. I'd love to stay."

I remembered my first day back, and a smile broke across my face. "He did?" I looked over at Jim. "Thanks, Jim."

He nodded.

"Alright. You two keep at it, and I'll have dinner in a jiffy." I pulled out the panini sandwich grill I bought on sale last month and a pot for the soup.

After the laughter died down, low murmurs about what pieces went where took its place. I looked over at Jim. He was so relaxed and happy.

Mini-Coop woke up and sat next to me. He wasn't one to beg, but he couldn't take his eyes off the cheese slices as I placed them on the bread. I broke off a piece for him and added the sandwiches to the grill and closed the press. The soup was just as easy. I added butter and fresh tomatoes to the pot with a little garlic, no-salt blend, and pepper. Then I filled it halfway with a mix of water and broth. I turned on the heat and blended everything with an immersion blender.

Vicky looked up from the puzzle. "How'd your outing with Shirley go?"

"It was really nice. I got a tour of the retirement community, met two nice ladies, and got a sneak peek at Shirley's new house. It's really cute."

"I have a few friends and clients that live there. Everyone raves about it."

"I can see why. It's pretty impressive. Jim, I hope you don't mind, I volunteered your muscles again to help Shirley box up her house and then to help her unpack. She's got a moving company to move the heavy furniture. She's going to have to sell most of it because her new place is half the size of her current home."

Jim did his famous muscle man flex. "Happy to be of service."

I turned off the heat from the soup and opened the grille press. "Do you guys want to take this conversation to the dining room since the puzzle's claimed the kitchen table?"

Vicky jumped up. "Let me help you with that."

"Thanks."

Vicky grabbed the plates.

I turned to Jim. "Hon, can you set the glasses on the table? We'll be right behind you."

"Yes, Captain." Jim set three glasses on a tray and made his way to the dining room.

I looked at his retreating back and waited until he was gone. I poured the soup bowls while Vicky placed the sandwiches on the plates. "Vicky, how'd he do today?"

"He had a great time. He asked about you more than usual and kept asking when you were coming home. I distracted him with the puzzle, and it triggered so many stories about riding horses as a kid he completely forgot you weren't there. Did anything happen this morning?"

I looked over her shoulder to make sure Jim hadn't returned. "Jim didn't want to take a shower and finally admitted he forgot how to work the knobs."

"Was he upset? How'd you handle it?"

"He was more sad than upset. I started it for him, but he still didn't want to take one. He didn't like the spray on his face. I thought about the group and remembered to give options. Of course, he shot down using a spa day that worked so well for William's wife. I resorted to trying out a new manly soap and offered to hold the sprayer."

"That's thinking on your feet. Did it work?"

"It did. Did he say anything to you? At first, he seemed so sad about admitting he didn't know how to turn on the shower, but by the time he was done, he was in a better mood."

"You did great. That's what the group is about. Learning from each other."

I tried not to cry again. "Does it mean he's going to get a lot worse?"

"It means he forgot how to turn on the shower. Remember, one day at a time. You handled it without stressing him or you out. That's what's important. Tomorrow, well, you'll figure out what works for tomorrow. Every day is different."

"I know. Thanks. Let's get in there before the soup gets cold."

Vicky grabbed a tray for the plates and water carafe, and I grabbed one for the soup bowls. I placed napkins, and spoons on my tray and we joined Jim in the dining room.

Chapter 45 Jim

I took my second cup of coffee on the porch while Jill vacuumed the house. The noise was like sitting next to a jet engine, and I couldn't stand it another second. I waved to the neighbors walking their dog. At least I think they were neighbors. I didn't recognize them. On second thought, they had to be because they knew my name. The small white fluffy dog bounced on all four feet, barking with such vigor I thought he wanted to eat me for breakfast. They apologized for his manners and made their way down the sidewalk, pulling him behind them while he gave me his last piece of mind.

I thought about the pup's excessive barking. He was protecting what was his, what he perceived were his parents? Was he claiming the sidewalk? The neighborhood? Who knew? Looking at him, he was the cutest little… I couldn't place the kind of pup, but I knew how he felt. I tried to suppress the rage building in me. My inner pup wanted to bark at Jill, at everyone. I wanted to bounce on all four feet and claim my house, claim my memory, claim my body. To tell everyone I was mad and scared. I wanted to hold on to the life I'd built.

I rocked my chair and looked at the homes on my street. It wouldn't be long before we'd be putting up a for sale sign. We had a nice dinner with Vicky last night. I couldn't remember all the conversation or the details about Shirley's new home. But I remember watching Jill trying to contain her excitement when she shared her visit to Shirley's new home, but she couldn't control her eyes lighting up. The part of me that stuffed down my inner pup from barking knew we would eventually need to move to the retirement community. She needed more support than Vicky's visit provided. It wouldn't hurt us to build a network of support sooner than later. We learned that from our group.

I don't know why I wanted to resist this next inevitable phase. The last thing I wanted was to be a burden or more of a burden. What was I trying to hold on to? It wasn't like I was going to remember the main drag to the house was just a dirt road or my house was one of the first homes in the development or that the large oak trees were just saplings lining the streets. Memories that would make a normal person want to hold on to the last vestiges of the life they built. Now there were over five thousand homes in the development, and the dirt road was a four-lane highway. Maybe it was time to let someone else's memories fill this brick-and-mortar building? Mine were seeping through all the cracks and crevices. Was that fair to the home?

I tried to mirror Jill's strength in all of this. At least her positive attitude. On most days, I could. Not discounting her constitution, but I think it was easier when it wasn't happening to you. My pulse quickened. I just realized why I wasn't ready to leave my home. It wasn't because of the memories. Selling this home would be admitting defeat. Living here, I could still hold on to the gratitude for all the good moments, celebrate the wins. Would I have the same strength and determination to keep fighting the progression if part of my brain and heart felt I'd admitted defeat by moving into the retirement community?

It wouldn't be fair to Jill to hold us back. I had to shift my focus, my perspective. We'd make new friendships that would help Jill as I progressed. I wanted that more than anything. Why couldn't I continue to fight the progression living somewhere else? Wouldn't it be easier with more resources?

Chapter 46 Jill

Mini-Coop dashed after his new playmate like a greyhound chasing a rabbit at the track. To the right of us, a border collie jumped high in the air after a frisbee, oblivious to the chase going on around him. His owner, a woman in her mid-thirties wearing a bright red tracksuit and matching running shoes, with curly brown hair, looked concerned at first, but when she realized we had our full attention on him, she relaxed and continued to play with her fur baby. This was our second off-leash park in the past few weeks. The last off-leash park, which was specifically designed for smaller pups, had asked our energetic boy to leave.

I actually liked this park better. It was larger and full of trees that would help shade the pups in the heat of the summer. Plus, the owners here were less snooty and chatted with each other. In the small-breed play area, they were either reading or taking 'important calls' on their phones, and if they took the time to look up from either of those tasks, it was to judge. I looked around at the expansive park. The dogs were as varied as their owners. There was a good mix of owners chatting amongst themselves as well as a few ball throwers and trainers. Owners and dogs of all ages and sizes. A nice mix.

I liked that this playground had agility equipment. Not a lot, but a few pieces to keep the more energetic dogs happy. There didn't seem to be any toy aggression over the scattering of dog balls, ropes, and squeaky toys. As I listened to the surrounding laughter, I was glad the other dog park had booted us. We would have never thought to come here, as it was farther from the house. Mini-Coop didn't earn the label "aggressive", but his energy was a bit overwhelming and off-putting, especially for the owners of smaller breeds.

So, here we were with our half-pint on the heels of a Great Dane. Mid-run, the huge dog did a swift about face, and our small furry friend stopped in his tracks and performed his best play bow, wiggling butt held high wagging his tail, letting his new buddy know his intentions were honorable, and all of his growling, barking, and snapping at the Dane's heels was just good old-fashioned fun. The new companion reciprocated by extending his huge paw across our boy's little shoulder, gently rolling him to his side. Then, with tenderness not to hurt our pup, he lowered himself and placed his great enormous head beside our pup's and started cleaning his tiny ears. Mini-Coop didn't move a muscle and seemed to enjoy the bath. When our little guy felt the arm relax, he eased himself from underneath and climbed aboard the big guy and licked his face and ears. Then they were both up and running again, the best of friends.

Jim and I sat on a bench and watched a little girl in pigtails run around with her Shih Tzu-poodle mix. Her dad, a man in his forties, dressed in a casual white shirt and jeans, would occasionally look up from his book and wave at her.

Jim looked concerned. "Are you sure we shouldn't take our little guy to the park for smaller pups?"

"Our little toot got kicked out, babe. They said he was too high-strung. He scared the smaller guys." I pointed to Mini-Coop rounding the corner behind the Great Dane. "He can hold his own with the larger guys. We just need to keep an eye on him." I rested my hand on Jim's leg to settle his anxiety. "Don't worry."

"He is holding his own. I love that little guy. Are they going to let him move in with us?"

"He's already living with us. Help me understand what you mean, move in with us."

"When we move where Shirley lives. I'm okay to move."

I leaned my body towards him and quickly reassured him. "Jim, we are nowhere near ready to move where Shirley lives. We're just fine where we are. I didn't mean to make you think we were moving. Did I upset you?"

Jim dropped his head, his smile faded. "I can move if you need to. I don't want things to be hard for you. I don't want you to move out."

"I'm not moving out. We're not moving. First, we can get help with the house and yard and maybe explore options to get help with you if I need it. We can do all of that before we ever need to move out. That's what Shirley did. There's so much we can do before we get to that stage. Okay?"

He didn't answer but continued to watch our pup. I could see the worry on his face despite my reassurance that we weren't going to move. I started to share we couldn't afford to move into a retirement home, at least not for another five or six years. We'd outlive our funds if we moved in too soon. Somehow, I didn't think he'd find that comforting.

Mini-Coop stopped off at the dog fountain for a drink and bounded over to us. He jumped on the bench next to Jim and kissed his cheek.

Jim laughed and pulled him in for a hug. "You're a pile of dirt. You need a bath, little guy."

I sent a silent thanks to our fur baby for breaking the tension.

Chapter 47 Jill

I'd never been to Shirley's before. We'd always met at the
park or at restaurants. Her neighborhood comprised a mixture of high-end, one-story ranch homes each one custom
with perfectly manicured landscapes. It didn't surprise me
she had a green thumb. The white front porch overflowed
with potted plants in full bloom, bringing a burst of color to
the entrance.

I started to knock on the door, a beautiful rich mahogany wood polished to a high gleam that accentuated the
intricate carved details, when I saw Shirley peering through
one of the glass windows on either side of the door.

She welcomed us in.

"Hi. I'm Jim. It's nice to meet you," Jim said as he
handed her his coat.

She didn't miss a beat. "Hi. I'm Shirley. It's nice to
meet you. You guys are amazing to help me with this." She
grabbed my coat. "I was always volunteering my husband's
muscle when my friends had to move as well. I really appreciate this."

"Of course, we're more than happy to help," I said.

It didn't worry me, that he didn't remember meeting
Shirley. It was natural for him not to recognize members of
the group outside of our sessions, without their name tags
and the context of the building we met in. He had no frame
of reference.

As Jim and I entered, the elegant ambiance that surrounded us was very much Shirley's personality. The mar-
ble entryway reflected a warm, golden hue from the mid-
morning sunlight gently streaming in through the door's
glass panels.

Shirley hung our coats on a mahogany coat rack that
matched the design of the front door. "I've got movers for

the big stuff, but to save on costs, I'm doing the packing and unpacking."

I hugged her. "*We're* doing the packing and unpacking." I looked around at the piles of boxes, neatly labeled and stacked, populating the hallway and surrounding rooms. "It looks like you've been at it for days already. I guess the 'we' was over stating."

"I've been at it for weeks, actually, but there's plenty left. You've seen the new place. We're really downsizing." She pointed to our left, to a room piled high and deep with boxes along the walls. "Everything along the walls in the den is being donated, so those boxes won't be going."

Jim and I leaned toward the den. The spacious room had a minimalistic modern design; and not surprising, since Shirley was an art teacher, the walls displayed a beautiful collection of fine art to include a large, abstract painting with vibrant colors over a sleek dark brown leather sofa. There were four matching leather chairs arranged around the sofa. The far wall had a built-in bookshelf that covered the entire wall. She'd already taken out the books and cleaned the shelves. There were no electronics in the room which was clearly designed for conversation and relaxation. A sculptured coffee table with a glass top and two matching end tables tied the room together beautifully.

Shirley turned to Jim. "I'll need your help to get the boxes to the local shelters for donation." She motioned to the empty bookcase. "My daughter picked up the books already. They were his prized possession, and she wanted to keep them in the family. The books in his office that still need to be packed are more light pleasure reading and trade manuals. We'll be donating those. If you see anything you like, please keep a pile for yourself."

Jim nodded.

She continued. "Thanks. A few organizations are taking the furniture from the two guest rooms. That leaves Carl's office to pack up. I've already picked out a few of his favorite books to keep from his office, but the rest will need to be boxed and donated. I'm donating his furniture as well. Carl's writing days are over, I'm afraid. Jim, because of the weight of the books, his office is your mission if you choose to accept."

Jim gave her a salute. "I accept."

Shirley smiled. "I've assembled the boxes and piled them in his office. It's the first door to the right."

Jim made his way to the office.

"I'm ready for my orders, Captain."

"I filled the bathtub in my bedroom with the clothes I'll be donating. Can you take large lawn bags and fill them with the clothes and put them in the back of my car and trunk? I might need to fill yours as well. I haven't thinned out my closet in thirty years. Both guest bath tubs are full as well."

"Of course. There's a donation center near my house. Do you need me to get a receipt?"

"That would be great, thanks. There is a box of black heavy-duty bags next to each tub. Those should do the trick."

I inhaled and pointed my nose in the direction of the smell. "That is the most delicious smelling coffee. I'm not asking to take a break before I get started, but can I grab a cup and take it in back?"

"Where are my manners? Of course. Follow me."

Shirley led me to the kitchen. She leaned against the counter, exhausted. "I knocked the kitchen out this morning."

"Did you get up at the crack of dawn?" There were so many boxes labeled "kitchen/glasses" and "plates."

"Pretty much."

I looked out the kitchen window at her lush backyard with a beautiful water fountain. "I could stand here and do dishes all day. Would I be able to move if I had such an amazing view?"

"It is a beautiful view."

I reached for a coffee cup on the drying rack and poured a cup. I added cream when Jim rounded the corner.

"Uh, guys. I don't think you want to donate this?"

I looked at his hand. He was holding a large, thick leather-bound book with gems along the center and a catch lock on the top and bottom right-hand side that didn't require a key. He handed the journal softened by years of handling to Shirley.

"I didn't mean to pry, but it was so pretty. It's full of drawings, letters, and the first page has a… tree with names on it. I think you should keep it."

Shirley opened it. "It's Carl's handwriting and his work. I've never seen it." She looked through the letters. "It's our old love letters." Her voice trembled.

"You've done so much. You're exhausted. Why don't you grab a cup of coffee and take a break and enjoy the journal?"

"I know you just got here and there is so much to do, but I'd love to share his memories with you. Would you mind if we went through some of it together? It would make me so happy to share my Carl with you guys."

"If it's not too private," I said.

Shirley's eyes moved across the page as she read. "Okay, maybe not this part." She laughed. "It's our first date, and, well, he's pretty descriptive about how he felt about, well, let's just say wanting to get to know me more intimately."

We all laughed.

She turned the pages as tears fell. She showed us a picture of the two of them at the hospital bed holding their baby girl. "Aw, he was so upset they wouldn't let him in the room for the birth of our daughter, Heather." On the back he had written, "My heart was hers the moment she curled her tiny fingers around mine. I wanted the moment to last forever, but they had to take her back to the nursery."

Jim handed her back the photo. "That's a beautiful picture. Don't take this the wrong way, because you're still gorgeous, but you were a knockout. Were you a model?"

"Jim! For Pete's sake!" I said.

Shirley laughed. "That's very sweet. I was a model. I didn't have a long career of it. It's how I paid for college, and then later in life I did side jobs for extra money for things like braces for Heather until Carl's career took off. You both know what a teacher's salary pays."

We nodded.

Shirley turned the pages, smiling as she handed us photos of their lives together. As she tucked the photos back and flipped through the journal, her head snapped up. "Oh, my word."

"What is it?" I asked.

She turned several pages and then returned to the point that caught her attention. "This entry starts with a comment that he's just been diagnosed with dementia. The rest of the journal is paragraphs of what he was going through and what he didn't want to forget." Her eyes rapidly skimmed the pages. "The details range from memories of Heather and me to his family and even what his childhood bedroom looked like." She flipped through a few more pages. "He even describes what it felt like when he played high school football, what his college dorm looked like. The pages are his memoir." She closed the journal and used her sleeve to wipe the tears streaming down her face.

Jim rubbed her shoulders. "I'm sorry. I didn't mean for it to make you cry."

"You found a treasure. Of course, it's making me cry. I'm going to go through this and write it as a book and gift it to our daughter. She's going to love it. Especially with the photos included in the chapters. I can't thank you enough."

I was bawling right along with her.

Jim came over and hugged me. "Would you have liked a journal?"

"I know there are several members in the group doing video journals. Would you rather do that? We can do whatever you are comfortable with," I said.

"I can't spell worth a darn anymore. Let's create a video about whatever memories I have left."

I turned to Shirley. "You enjoy the journal and take your time. You've done so much. Let Jim and me pack up the rest. We'll take a break for lunch and you can share his memories. How does that sound?"

She sniffled. "It sounds lovely. Thank you both."

Jim and I headed to our respective rooms to help Shirley transition to her next home.

My heart soared. I had memories of our lives together, but from my perspective; I wish I had them from his, but maybe now with this video project, I'd get to know more of him. I had no idea the memories he didn't share, like his childhood bedroom, what he felt when he started a school for the first time. Those long-term memories were still intact. I was excited about getting to know young Jim.

Chapter 48 Jill

Jim and I walked under the "Colorful Minds: The Art of Living with Dementia" banner as we entered the bustling community center. We gave our tickets to a lovely young lady with dark purple hair dressed in black slacks and a white shirt. In exchange, she gave us a beautiful brochure about the Memory Café program. It had a brief description of each member's story behind each of the paintings they had submitted to the exhibit. I was familiar with it, as I helped edit the final piece. The writing was beautiful and inspired empathy and dedication to helping others. At first, we were going to use the exhibit as an outreach to the community, but each of the members decided to donate a painting to raise funds for the program. It was our way of giving back.

Jim squeezed my hand at the excitement of our support group's first public exhibition to raise awareness and funds. Something we'd hoped would become an annual event well beyond the five-year grant period. Janet's foundation was not only receiving donations for the cost to attend the event, but the attendees were bidding on the pieces submitted by the group. We made our way through the crowd to the exhibit area, admiring the sea of crisp tuxedos, bow ties, colorful gowns, and dazzling jewelry. It was fun to dress up. I couldn't remember the last time we'd attended a black-tie affair. The formal clothing against the colorful and expressive paintings was striking. Classical music played softly in the background, adding to the sophistication of the evening.

The gallery was breathtaking and professionally done. If I didn't know better, I'd have thought we were walking through an exhibit of renowned artists. Each work displayed the artist's name, bidding number, a narrative description of the piece, and noted if they were the caregiver or not. The paintings included landscapes, stills, portraits, and abstracts. Some were colorful, while a few were dark, all conveying emotions, sensations, or memories. The smell of candles and fresh-cut flower arrangements strategically placed brought any flowers in the paintings to life and created a relaxing atmosphere.

Jim and I accepted a plate of hors d'oeuvres to share and two iced teas. After saying hello and exchanging excited congratulations with the other members, we positioned ourselves in front of our paintings. Within minutes, a tall and very handsome man stopped short in front of Jim's landscape. The woman who had her arm linked with his almost collided into his shoulder. She was stunning with wide round eyes that sparkled like her diamond necklace under the lights. The most gorgeous red silk dress I'd ever seen hugged her curves. Of course, her hair and makeup were flawless. I felt underdressed with my simple black cocktail dress and single-strand pearl necklace.

"Did you paint that? Is that in Oirland?" he asked.

Jim looked back at his painting. "I don't remember painting it. But I know it's in Ireland. It's Mhamó's land. I used to love sitting on that brick wall watching the sheep. It drove Mom nuts. She'd always yell at me to get down before I cracked my head like Humpty Dumpty. Mhamó would always tell her, 'Let the boy be. Bones break, bones heal.'" He laughed.

I tried not to look surprised at the admission he didn't recall painting it. I nodded and smiled.

"Jaysus, that brings back memories. I miss my Mhamó. She reared me when my parents died. I could hear me Mhamó sayin' the same thing. She was a tough and sturdy woman and didn't pamper me at all. Made me the man I am today, God rest her soul." He extended his hand. "My name is Liam, and this is my wife, Samantha."

We shook hands. "It's a pleasure to meet you. Your grandmother sounds like a wonderful woman," I said.

"That she was, aye."

Samantha's green eyes welled with tears. "It's beautiful. All of your pieces are beautiful." She tucked a strand of her long chestnut hair behind her ear as she spoke. "My mother and both grandparents had Alzheimer's. She held up the brochure. Unfortunately, they didn't have such a beautiful support group to help them."

"The program's support and education have been a blessing through this journey. It's tough to do it alone. I can't imagine how hard it must have been for your family."

"It was. I was young, but I have strong memories of my mom trying to raise us kids at the same time she was taking care of both my grandparents. I always wondered if the stress of handling both at the same time is what triggered her early onset. I'm doing what I can to stay healthy and keep up on the latest research and advances should I follow in their footsteps. This event means a lot to me. I want to do what I can to help."

"I'll keep you in my prayers. I'm glad you are staying healthy. It's critical and has helped with Jim's progression, I'm certain of it."

"Thank you. I'll take all the prayers I can get." Liam put his arm around her and kissed the top of her head. I fought back tears and prayed she'd live a long, healthy life.

We heard the tapping of fingers against a mic. "Please join us in the grand ballroom."

Liam shook Jim's hand. "We'd best be sittin' down. May the luck o' the Irish be with ye all with the biddin'."

The members followed the attendees out of the exhibit area. We entered the ballroom. The front row was reserved for us artists, and we each took our seats, beaming with pride. David Richardson, the neurologist following our group, set up his father's piece next to the podium. His parents, Marg and Jack, helped him adjust the painting on the easel and then took their seats at the end of our row. Jack's painting was even more beautiful with the overhead spotlight accenting the vibrant colors.

Behind Richard, a video of our group laughing and moving to the music as we painted played on a loop.

Janet lifted the mic from the stand. "Good evening, my name is Janet Helver, and I'm the founder of a local nonprofit Memory Café program. Thank you so much for attending. I have no doubt you are here because your lives have been touched in some way by the devastating effects of dementia. As some of you may already know, it's a general term for several diseases that affect a person's memory, cognitive thinking, and their ability to perform daily tasks or activities."

Several heads nodded.

"Just a high-level note about our foundation. We have music programs, light exercise, caregiver peer support, and pet therapies. There's never a cost for the participants or care partners. We also provide stimulating programs, such as the art you see here. Aren't the pieces exquisite?" She waited for the claps to die down. "I hope you had a chance to walk around and pick your favorite piece or pieces to bid on during our first Colorful Minds: The Art of Living with Dementia exhibit. We were very *mindful*, yes, pun intended when we selected the name for the exhibit. I believe there's an art to living with dementia. The word I want to emphasize is *living*. If you take away one thing tonight ... besides your new painting"—everyone laughed.— "it's to shift the mindset that you or your loved ones have dementia, but instead are living with dementia. The difference? What you see here tonight is proof that you can live positively with dementia. My foundation helps to shift the focus on what participants can do instead of what skills are no longer possible. I believe that dementia is not the end of life, but a different way of living. Social programs, like my Memory Café, help participants and care partners find ways to cope with the challenges and changes this journey brings. We do it together with support from others who understand what we're going through. Despite the diagnosis, we live purposeful and productive lives."

Everyone clapped.

She waved at them. "You've got the brochure. If you are a caregiver or a person living with cognitive impairment, please reach out to the resources listed in the brochure for support, education, and resources. I won't take any more time away from why we are all here. The auction! I'll turn the mic over to Dr. David Richardson. He is a neurologist, as well as a family member of one of our esteemed artists, Jack Richardson. Thank you again for attending, and I hope you have a wonderful evening."

The room erupted with claps and whistles as David stepped up to the podium.

"Thank you. Thank you. I'm honored to receive such a warm welcome." His voice choked. He motioned to the painting next to him. "As some of you in the room already know, Dad hadn't touched a paintbrush in ten years before this painting. His prior paintings hung in galleries across the state and each one sold for thousands." His words hung heavy in the air as his gaze swept across the front row, his eyes landing on his dad before he continued. "My dad had been withdrawn for so many years, he and mom were isolated, their friends had either passed or weren't comfortable coming over to the house. Last year, I noticed his behavior, actually, both of their behaviors were more engaging and positive." He smiled at his mom. "Sorry, Mom, for airing the dirty laundry, but I came over for dinner one night and noticed she wasn't yelling at Dad. When I asked her about it, she told me about the support group and that she'd found a safe space to share her feelings and frustrations. She'd also learned how to manage her stress and anger. She told me in the past week she'd counted to ten more times than she could remember. She also learned to talk calmly and use gentle words. Remember that, Mom?"

His mother laughed and nodded as she looked around the audience.

"She said she stopped arguing with him and just entered his reality. It really shifted their communication and relationship."

He looked around the room. "Most recently, there was another shift when Mom and Dad started art and music therapy. I won't bore you with everything that's firing and wiring in the brain, but there's a lot going on when the brush hits the canvas. The visual cortex processes shapes, colors, and textures. As the brush moves, it stimulates the senses and can awaken memories and emotions.

"As I've witnessed with my own parents, it can also improve mood, self-esteem, and attention span. Combining music stimulates multiple regions of the brain. I've seen improvements in social interaction and emotional regulation. We have only just begun to explore this issue. I'll be studying the combination of art and music therapy over the next five years. It's promising. Not only did Dad regain his passion for painting, but I've seen improvement in his attention span."

He highlighted the role of art therapy in enhancing the brain's ability to rewire and adapt to new experiences. "As Janet said, I won't take any more time away from why we are all here: the auction!"

The video displayed the first painting with a number 1 on the upper right corner. He handed Janet the microphone.

"Thank you, David. Isn't he amazing! I'm looking forward to working with him and his amazing project. Speaking of art therapy, this beautiful piece here is a self-portrait created by Becky Harwell at her favorite vacation spot, Cannon Beach, Oregon. The details of her photos are in the brochure. Do I have an opening bid?"

A strong female voice came from the back of the room. "Six hundred dollars."

Before I could turn to see who had started the bidding, the numbers climbed: $700, $800, each in hundred dollar increments until a booming male voice shot up his bid card and yelled out, "Three thousand dollars!"

I regretted sitting in the front row. My neck was sore from turning to see the action.

Janet called out, "A beautiful start. Do I hear more?"

And more she did as the bidding continued. We all looked at each other in amazement.

Chapter 49 Jill

A year had passed since the auction, and the memory of that night still brought a smile to my face. The months had been a whirlwind of activity, but one thing stood out above all else: Jim's landscape had garnered the highest bid at two hundred thousand dollars. The stipulation stated that the funds would be earmarked for grants for care partners who could not afford respite care or at-home nursing care.

Liam bought the painting and then returned it to Jim. He said the donation was for his wife, Samantha, but the painting belonged to Jim. He loved the painting, as it brought back memories of his childhood, but he wanted it to stay with us. It represented Jim's memory of his grand-mother and needed to stay in the family. Jim beamed as we hung it over the fireplace. We exchanged Christmas cards, a tradition I hoped would continue. She would remain in my prayers. They both would.

The glow of the fire danced on the delicate blown glass ornaments as I hung them on the branches. I put the last ornament on the red and white Christmas tree as Jim stood close by, looking out the window, watching the snow fall. Mini-Coop was fast asleep on his bed next to the fire. The sounds of his soft breath mixed in with the crackling fire. This year, I didn't have to fight back tears as I hung all the quirky and sentimental ornaments we had collected over the years. This year, I happily hummed to the Christmas songs playing from the overhead speakers instead of using it as a mental distraction. I thought about everything we went through since the diagnosis. I no longer felt lost, heartbroken, and alone. Instead, I felt supported and grate-ful for the moments of joy and connection. With the help of the support group and Vicky, I found the resilience to carry us both through to the end.

With the tree complete, I placed the sparkly wooden "Believe" sign on the fireplace mantel, and tucked spruce garland, pine cones, red berries, and glitter around the sign. The room was once again taking shape into my favorite winter wonderland. I tossed red and white Christmas pillows on the couch and placed a Christmas throw over the back.

I picked up a book from the end table. "Jim, why don't you join me? I picked out your favorite book."

"I have a favorite?"

"It changes. This one was your favorite last month. I can read a few chapters, and if you don't like it, I can grab another. How does that sound?"

He sat next to me but said nothing. He was still relatively healthy. His communication had slowed to minimal words unless it was a good day. I relied on body language for most of his responses on the not-so-good days.

I opened the book and felt the weight of my wedding ring as I held the pages open. It felt good to wear it again. I'd put it back on a few months after the exhibit. The day he remembered Cooper was our pup after seeing my painting, I knew at a high level he knew there was an "us" and that we were married, even though he didn't remember our wedding or details of our lives together. One evening he was curious as to why he had a wedding ring on and I didn't. He asked me if I didn't wear mine because he'd forgotten we were married. His comment caught me off guard. The only thing I could think of was to tell him I was worried about getting paint on it during one of our sessions and forgot to put my ring back on. I went to my jewelry box and returned proudly wearing it. He was satisfied. I never took it off after that. A few months later, he asked to see our wedding photos. He was sad that he didn't remember being married but wasn't upset. He accepted it was a part of the disease.

After that, I slowly hung our photos back up around the house. I thank God he never remembered that horrible night he kicked me out. If I had to rank the value of all the lessons I learned, entering his world instead of forcing him back into reality was number one. There were a few occasions he mistook me for his sister. When he did, I entered his reality, and we enjoyed stories of their childhood. There were a few stories I wasn't familiar with, but I used my imagination to fill in the gaps. Only once did he think I was Melinda. He called me Melinda on more than one occasion, but I don't think he ever thought I was really her. Except for one time when he acted like I was home for the holidays and asked me how I liked living in England. He asked me if I would ever come back to the States. I felt horrible, but I told him England was my home and didn't see myself returning. He just nodded, as if he already knew the answer before he asked.

The crackling of the fire pulled me out of my thoughts, and I felt Jim shifting in the chair beside me, a yawn escaping his lips. I tucked the throw around us, the soft fabric covering us in warmth. He placed his head on my shoulder, a comforting weight bringing me to the present.

I cleared my throat. "Chapter 1.

Dear Reader,

I hope you enjoyed *The Nurse*, a story that is incredibly close to my heart. If you or a loved one are dealing with dementia, please know that you are not alone. I wish you strength, courage, and resilience on your journey. Remember to reach out for support when you need it and prioritize self-care. You can't pour from an empty cup.

If this book resonated with you, I would be grateful if you could help keep the conversation going about dementia and the importance of self-care for caregivers. Please follow *The Nurse* on social media and consider watching the short film that inspired me to expand Jill and Jim's journey into this novel. Sharing your thoughts and experiences can make a world of difference for others navigating similar challenges.

If you feel inclined, I would sincerely appreciate a review on Amazon. Your honest feedback helps other readers discover this book and supports my work as an author. However, I kindly ask that you remember there is a human being at the other end of your words. While this book may not be everyone's cup of tea, I poured my heart into telling a story that although fiction, is a testament to the unbreakable bonds of love, the resilience of the human spirit, and the profound truth that even when memories fade, the heart never forgets. Thank you for taking the time to read *The Nurse*. Your support means the world to me.

With gratitude,

Joyce Kostakis

Two beginnings, one timeless love

The Nurse Trailer   The Nurse Short Movie

The Nurse Facebook   The Nurse Instagram